LIGHT MY FIRE

J. KENNER

M&O

Light My Fire

by

J. Kenner

About Light My Fire

I don't do relationships.

I've lived my life hiding my scars, revealing myself only the in the scripts I write and the characters I voice.

Few people know the real me. I'm too careful. Too afraid of getting burned all over again.

Enter Beverly Martin. A movie star. A woman so beautiful and caring she makes my heart ache. She says she wants me—and her touch almost makes me believe that a girl like her could love a man like me.

But being with her would mean letting the spotlight of fame shine on me, too. And I'm not sure I can do that—even if walking away means losing the woman I love.

Meet Mr. November — winter's about to get hot!

Each book in the series is a STANDALONE with NO cliffhanger and a guaranteed HEA!

But even so, you won't want to miss any in the series. Because then you can answer the question…

Who's Your Man of the Month?

Down On Me
Hold On Tight
Need You Now
Start Me Up
Get It On
In Your Eyes
Turn Me On
Shake It Up
All Night Long
In Too Deep

Light My Fire
Walk The Line

and don't miss Bar Bites: A Man of the Month
Cookbook!

Visit manofthemonthbooks.com to learn more!

Chapter One

"COULD YOU REPEAT THAT?" Griffin Draper drew a deep breath, not quite able to process film producer Matthew Holt's incredible announcement.

Had he really said, "Sold?"

Was Griffin's script actually going to become a movie?

Too stunned to think straight, Griff dropped down onto the overstuffed couch in the twentieth-floor conference room of Bender, Twain & McGuire's Austin office, where Griffin and Beverly Martin had been asked to come meet Holt and Griffin's entertainment attorney, Evie Morrison.

The moment Griffin sat, Beverly did the same, settling in right next to him, only a few inches of air separating him from the dark-haired actress's hypnotic beauty.

He forced himself not to scoot away from her even as he told himself that the tightness in his gut was the result of nerves about Holt's news—*not* about her. He might be attracted to her—what man wouldn't be?—but since there was nothing between them, and there never would be, why the hell would he be nervous?

Sure, they'd become friends, but even that had developed slowly. Mostly because he'd kept his distance since, dammit, he'd been attracted to her from the first moment she'd settled down on a barstool next to him about five months ago in May. But that attraction was tainted with the knowledge that he couldn't have her. Ever.

Story of his life, right?

But at least his personal torment had inspired a good screenplay.

The thought brought him back to the present and to Matthew—the Hollywood wunderkind known for his serious expression and no-nonsense manner —who now stood in front of Griffin, sporting an uncommon hint of a grin.

"Lost in dreams of the red carpet premiere already?"

"Would you blame me?" Griff quipped. "But, seriously. I need you to say that again."

Beside him, Beverly shifted but remained silent. In front of him, Matthew's smile widened. "You heard me, cowboy. Apex Studios is a go. They're putting everything behind *Hidden Justice*, and unless we go seriously off the rails, filming will begin in Vancouver in the spring. For a release the following summer."

"I can't——" The words caught in his throat. It was all too much.

"Congratulations, Griff." Evie Morrison, his attorney, hadn't said much during the meeting, even though the conference was taking place in the Austin office of the LA-based law firm where she worked. Now, she looked like she was about to explode with delight for him. "I'll be back in LA tomorrow, and I'm getting together with Van to go over the deal points," she added, referring to Griff's manager. "It's really happening."

Beside him, Beverly flashed the bright, sweet smile that had become famous all across America. "Congrats, Griff. Not that I'm at all surprised. I told you it was a winner."

An Austin native, Beverly Martin had recently starred in a quirky independent drama that had hit the current American zeitgeist perfectly. *Suburban Love Song* had racked up all sorts of awards, and Beverly had suddenly found herself sheathed in a cloak of fame.

From what Griffin had seen, she wore her fame well. Serious about her career and smart about her choices, Beverly continued to live primarily in Texas, and she'd done only one other project since her debut—a smart and edgy thriller that was set to release in about a week. She'd let Griffin read the script—which was brilliant—and had promised to get him an early DVD of the film.

Now, she leaned forward. "Who's directing?" she asked Holt.

"Christopher Deaver. He all but begged."

"Really?" Griffin turned to Beverly, whose smile had widened. "He directed the one coming out next week, right? *Crypto Games?*

"He did." She looked positively radiant at the news,

and Griff's gut tightened. Not with jealousy, of course. How could he be jealous? It was only that he was the odd man out, having never met Deaver.

"That's the best news," Beverly said to Holt and Evie before turning her attention back to Griff. "He's got a real talent for edginess and suspense. We couldn't ask for a better director for a project like this."

As she spoke, she casually reached out, then closed her left hand over Griffin's right. Griff fought the urge to flinch as he reminded himself that she couldn't feel anything. As usual, his hand was mostly concealed by the sleeve of the overlarge hoodie-style sweat jacket he habitually wore. So there was no way she could feel the rough, horrible scars. No way she could tell that he only had a nub for a pinkie finger.

He told himself that … and at the same time, he casually shifted on the couch, pulling his hand away as he did so, then stretching in what he hoped was a nonchalant manner.

Looking sideways, he saw Beverly press her lips together as she moved her hand to her lap. Yeah, she was one hell of an actor, because if she was embarrassed or annoyed, it didn't show at all. And the truth was, he actually wanted to hold her hand. Wanted a physical connection between them during this incredible moment—a moment that belonged to both of them. After all, none of this would be happening if she weren't attached to star in the movie.

Except that he didn't go for physical. He never shook hands in greeting—people habitually extended their right hand, and that sure as hell wasn't going to happen. Plus, he didn't hug or do air-kisses, because why the hell would he get close enough for someone to get a good look at his face?

The only exception was Kelsey, and that wasn't even because she was his sister. Instead, it was because she carried much the same scars as he did —hers just didn't show. She'd been babysitting him the night it happened, making him promise to be good and to keep her secret while she snuck out for a date. He'd been almost thirteen, old enough to stay home alone and stupid enough to believe he knew everything. He'd wanted to toast marshmallows on the outside grill and make s'mores.

Now he couldn't look at the things without throwing up.

The last thing he remembered was that he'd used gasoline from the toolshed when he'd had trouble lighting the grill.

He'd awakened in a hospital days later, his right side raw with fourth-degree burns that blanketed him in a pain so red and vile that all the narcotics in the world couldn't dull it. It had been his fault. *All* his fault. But Kelsey blamed herself, and now she was just as scarred as he was.

He'd done that to her. Wounded her heart. And now he carried that guilt, along with his scars.

Beside him, Beverly sat stiffly, her fingers twined together in her lap, and her attention on Holt instead of Griffin.

"I knew you'd be pleased about Deaver," Holt told Beverly. "He was thrilled when he heard you were already attached." His brow furrowed as he squinted at her. "You are still attached, right?"

"Don't even joke around," she said. "You know I am. I practically hogtied Griff and refused to leave him alone until he let me stake my claim as Angelique."

"You hardly had to twist my arm," Griff reminded

her when she turned to face him once again, her bright, earnest expression reminding him of their first meeting.

"What happened?" Evie asked.

"Only me making a complete ass of myself," Beverly said. "It was a few months ago in spring, and my agent called to tell me about this incredible script that she wasn't supposed to have. Sorry about that," she added as an aside to Griff.

"All things considered, I'm gonna say it wasn't a problem. Van's friends with Evelyn Dodge," he explained to Evie. "And Evelyn is Beverly's agent."

"Van was so excited about the script when he read the first draft," Beverly said, picking up the story, "that he slipped it to Evelyn without asking Griffin."

"Evelyn liked what she read," Griffin continued, "and she thought that Beverly would be perfect for the role of Angelique. So she shot a copy of the first draft to Bev." He sighed and shook his head. "It's probably a good thing she didn't tell me, because I would've completely freaked and told her not to do it. The idea of landing Beverly Martin would have intimidated the hell out of me, and I would have held back the script until it was polished to within an inch of its life."

"Are you kidding?" Bev leaned sideways to casually shoulder bump him. "It was brilliant, and I went nuts over it. I actually read it in my car in Evelyn's driveway. I didn't intend to, but I decided to peek and see if it really was as special as she said. I read it twice, then marched back to her door, pounded until she let me in, and told her I'd do whatever it took to get the role."

Evie laughed. "Did she know you were out there in her driveway?"

"Not a clue. She'd pulled me aside at a small cock-tail party she was throwing. By the time I went back to the door, everyone had gone home, and I caught her in sweatpants and no makeup. She wasn't going to let me in—I called her cell phone from her front porch—but when I told her I had to have the role, she ushered me in and we connived."

Griffin's brows rose. "Connived?"

"Well, you know I came back to Austin and made a point of meeting you at The Fix. But have I ever mentioned that I'd planned on staying in LA through the summer?"

He leaned toward her. "What? No. Why?"

"No particular reason. A friend was heading to London and offered me his place, and Chris said he'd teach me to sail." She shrugged. "But then I realized that coming home to Austin made a whole lot more sense."

"Chris," Griffin repeated. "You mean Deaver. Your director."

She nodded. "Yeah, we became pretty close during the shoot. Like I said, he's a great guy. You'll like him."

Not jealous, Griff reminded himself. *Really not jealous.*

He sucked in a breath. "So instead of staying in LA with him, you came to Austin for me."

Crap. Had he truly said that out loud?

Thankfully, the words seemed to roll right off Bev, although when Griff caught Holt's eye, he thought the other man's expression seemed a little too knowing.

"I did," she said, then focused her attention on Evie again. "Turns out that the studio that produced

Suburban Love Story is also producing Griff's web series. And it's based in Austin."

Griffin had moved to Austin about two years ago, partly to get away from the LA grind and that city's obsession with appearance. He'd been making a name as a voice actor, but any type of acting in Los Angeles required meetings, public appearances, and just generally being seen. While he loved the work, he much preferred to stay in his cave writing his popular podcast and recording the episodes.

So when the Austin company had optioned the podcast for a web series, it made sense to make the move to Texas.

Now, his web series was up and running and hugely successful. He hadn't been convinced that something on the Internet could really be monetized, but he'd been proven wrong when he'd seen the first check. The process of converting the podcast to a web series had also made him realize how much he enjoyed the writing process, and that was when he'd started to focus on *Hidden Justice*, a script he'd outlined almost entirely at The Fix.

"I wondered how you knew to find me at The Fix," he told Beverly.

She winked at Evie. "I stalked him. Ended up basically accosting him at the bar. And he's such a gentleman he even bought me a drink."

"Yeah, but I do that for every beautiful woman who tells me she loves my script." That was a lie. He never bought women drinks. That was a ritual that led down a path he never traveled. He still had no idea what prompted him to signal Cam to bring her a glass of wine. Had he simply been flattered that she liked his script? Or had he been hoping for something more?

"I was shameless," Beverly continued, unaware of the direction of his thoughts. "Told him it was brilliant. After a few drinks, I told him *he* was brilliant. And I said that I wanted to be attached, and if he told me I wasn't what he had in mind, I'd have to go lay down in front of one of the horse-drawn carriages they pull tourists around in."

"I didn't believe her," he said. "But I didn't want to risk it. So I said yes. Seemed like the best choice at the time."

"I love that story," Evie said. "So you two decided to start working together on the script?"

"Oh, no!" Beverly said. "Griffin doesn't need my

help. I'm just giving him a little bit of an actress's perspective, and urging him along."

"She's being modest, Griffin said. "She's been a huge help. I wasn't expecting it, but we make a good team."

Beverly tilted her head as she turned to him, her eyes soft as they studied him. "Yes," she said softly, "we do."

Griffin felt that tightening in his gut again. That sparkle in his soul. He knew he needed to ignore it. Knew that there was only friendship between them. But even so, wisps of memory kept taunting him. The way they laughed when they worked together. The fire in her eyes when she was passionate about a line. The sweet bells of her laughter when she teased him.

And every one of those memories was bittersweet because each one brought on a craving that he couldn't satisfy. A longing that would never be fulfilled.

But that didn't change the wishing.

Thank goodness the script was polished and done, because each time she came over to review the script or discuss the characters was sweet torment. At least they were busy—no time to talk about their pasts or what they wanted, or life in general. No time to really get close.

As far as Griffin was concerned, that was a good thing. He needed to keep his distance. And lately, the ache of unfulfilled desire for this woman was becoming more and more painful. Which was why he was so damn relieved that the script was done, it was going to a studio, and he could get clear of Beverly at least long enough to draw a deep breath and push his own reset button.

"So now we wait, right?" he asked Holt. "They've got Bev attached, but they'll start talking with other actors and—"

"All true. Except for the waiting part. They have notes." Holt looked between him and Beverly. "Mostly about Angelique. They want her role beefed up, and they specifically want Bev in on the revisions. They love the script, don't get me wrong, but they intend this movie to be a star vehicle."

He flashed a broad smile at both of them. "In other words, this project has the potential to catapult you both to the next level."

"Oh," Beverly said, as Griffin's stomach did a brand new series of somersaults.

"I'll schedule a call for tomorrow and we can go over everything, but then they need the revisions back in a week. Ten days max if we're going to do this thing."

"Do this thing?" Griff repeated. "But I thought it was a done—"

"We're on it," Beverly said. "Hell, I'll move into Griff's place if I need to."

Griff frowned. "I don't think—"

"I'll call Donovan at Apex after we're done," Holt said. "I'll tell him how excited you are."

"You won't be lying," Griff said as Beverly reached over to squeeze his right hand.

He stood up like a shot, in the process tugging his hand free. *Excited?* Yeah, that was a fair assessment of the situation.

She rose as well. "I'd like to prepare for tomorrow. Maybe go over the script together and break down Angelique's scenes?"

"Um, yeah. Sure." He glanced at his watch. "You

have to be at The Fix in a few hours, though." Tonight was a Man of the Month contest, and this time the crowd would be choosing Mr. October. The bar had started having the contest as a way to bring in more customers, and it had worked like a charm.

Griff knew the female customers came to see the parade of shirtless men, but as far as Griff was concerned, the biggest draw was the emcee— Beverly had been hosting the contest since the beginning. And knowing what he now did about how she came back to Austin to meet him, Griff couldn't help but wonder if she'd accepted the job as a way to stay close.

If that was the case, he knew it was only about the script. Even so, the thought pleased him more than it should.

Tonight, Griffin had a reason other than Beverly to go. His personal trainer Matthew Herrington was entered. And on top of that, following the contest, The Fix intended to air the series premiere of *The Business Plan* on their big screen televisions. A real estate reality show, the program documented the bar's remodel and included bits from the bi-weekly calendar guy contest.

Considering how close he'd become to the owners, staff, and regulars, Griff didn't intend to miss any of that.

Beverly looked up from where she was tapping something out on her phone. "Megan's going to bring her case to The Fix and do my makeup there. That means I don't have to leave your place until six. So we have plenty of time. I'll meet you there?"

Apparently, he was all out of excuses. "Sure. Give me an hour or so head start. I need to clean up." Or, more accurately, he needed time to make sure he was in control before he sat at his computer with Beverly behind him, her breath on the back of his neck.

Maybe he should invest in a second monitor...

She leaned closer, her hand going to his shoulder as she leaned in. "We did it," she whispered. "*You* did it."

Maybe so. But there was still a long way to go.

He hoped he could focus. Because God knew being next to Beverly was really starting to mess with his head.

Chapter Two

BEVERLY SMILED as she eased out of her sunshine yellow Volkswagen Beetle, now parked in front of Griffin's East Austin bungalow. He might be frustrated by the prospect of more revisions, but Beverly wasn't. She was determined to make sure that the script was so perfect that not even the most jaded studio exec could turn it down, and if that meant sacrificing a few hours to work on the screenplay, then those were hours she'd happily donate to the cause.

The movie, however, was just an excuse for her good mood. The truth was much more simple—and more complicated. Because her smile was all about Griffin. And Griffin was as complicated as they came.

She hummed as she climbed the steps to the porch. A charming space, it was surrounded by a wooden railing and was immaculately swept, with pots of colorful flowers lining the perimeter and two bright blue wooden rocking chairs sitting on either side of a tiled mosaic table.

A crape myrtle planted beside the patio provided dappled shade and brilliant color. And a twisting vine of wild mustang grapes climbed one of the support pillars, adding a hint of rebellion to the otherwise tidy porch.

She'd been here dozens of times over the last few months, and each time she climbed these steps, Beverly couldn't help but think about how much Griff and the house fit each other. Like Griffin, the house was a survivor. He'd told her that when he'd bought it two years ago, it had been a wreck, essentially ripped apart by the strung-out renters who'd cooked meth in the detached garage, then sampled their own product inside the house. They'd let the place turn to shit, and when they'd been arrested, the landlord decided he'd had enough. He put the house on the market confident that such a wreck would never sell. Or, if it did, it would be a tear down.

But Griff had seen the potential. He bought the place, put in the work, and turned it into a shining star that kept its original charm and character.

"How did you find a contractor?" she'd asked. She'd recently bought a 1950's cottage by the lake and was thinking about renovations.

"I did most of the work myself," he'd told her.

"Nice. I wish I'd grown up knowing how to do that. Handy skills to have."

It wasn't until a few months later when they knew each other better that she learned that he hadn't gone into the project with any particular skills. Just a willingness to learn and a desire to make the house fit his vision of what it should be. "I taught myself how to work on classic cars when I was a teenager. Honestly, I figured a house would probably be easier."

She'd shaken her head, more awed than surprised. After all, by that time, she knew him pretty well. She'd watched him focus for hours on a script, witnessed his process of building a character, ensuring that the people he was writing for the screen were just that—*people*. Not mere words and descriptions on the page, little more than cardboard cutouts designed to speak the lines.

He did the work that needed to be done. On his script. On his house. Even down to all the pretty flowers that brightened his patio.

And somehow, in all of that, he still found time to not only work on a Mustang he was rebuilding, but to keep up with a strict regimen of personal training. That much she'd learned by snooping. She'd become friends with Matthew Herrington—a regular at The Fix and one of the contestants in tonight's Man of the Month calendar contest—and he'd happened to mention that Griffin was one of his personal training clients.

That overarching drive was one of the things that Beverly liked most in Griffin, and that admiration had only grown as she'd gotten to know him better.

Now, maybe, she liked him a little bit too much. Because Bev was the kind of woman who went after the things she wanted. And lately, she'd come to realize that what—*who*—she wanted was Griffin.

But she had a feeling that if she went after him, she'd only end up pushing him away.

"Get a grip, Martin," she muttered to herself, waiting to ring the doorbell until after she pressed the pad of her right thumb into the fleshy part at the base of her left. It was an old habit, taught to her by her very first acting coach after she'd bombed five auditions in a row.

"Pretend you're me," he'd said. "And you're shaking like a leaf, too scared to get your bony little butt out on that stage. I'd tell you to get a grip, wouldn't I? Well, this is how you do it."

She'd been twelve, and he'd shown her how to hold her hands together so that she could grip that one pressure point hard. She didn't know if it was some sort of eastern medicine, acupuncture, or just a mind trick. She didn't care, either. She'd taken his advice, then went out and won her very first speaking role in a local commercial for one of Austin's car dealerships.

Ready now, she jammed her thumb against the button, then heard the familiar chime echoing behind the cornflower blue door. Without thinking about it, she stood a little straighter, wanting to look her best for when he answered the door. Ridiculous, of course, but she couldn't help the way she felt. And as she waited for him to let her in, she let her mind drift back to the first time she'd become aware of Griffin Blaize.

Everyone in Hollywood knew about the voice actor who had made a splash with his podcast. And once Beverly had read his script, she wanted to learn everything she could about the man who had captured her imagination.

Evelyn, her agent, knew people close to Griffin, including his brother-in-law, Wyatt Segel, and Bev felt justified in asking for a few more details about the man she was determined to work with.

When she learned that he'd been horribly burned as a child, she appreciated the humor that went along with his pen name. As if he was flipping the bird to that damn fire.

Tears had stung her eyes when she learned that his burns were extensive, covering essentially all of the right side of his body. And she'd wept openly when Evelyn had told her that the burns had impacted more than his appearance. That they were, in fact, so extensive that his muscles had been severely damaged, resulting in both a limited range of motion and significant chronic pain.

Only a few people in Hollywood knew the truth.

Directors and producers with whom he'd worked, his manager, and a few others. When Beverly learned, her heart broke for the little boy he'd once been, a child who must have been terrified and in desperate pain.

And as she came to know him, her heart longed to heal the man, even as she admired so much about his skill and talent and perseverance.

No doubt about it, Beverly had fallen for him. For this fascinating man who buried himself fully in every project, and yet still managed to find the time to deadhead his potted flowers and make his home so welcoming.

And it wasn't only that she admired Griffin's talent. The truth was, she was wildly attracted to him. She knew damn well that he'd never believe it, but there was something so deliciously sensual about his eyes, brown with golden flecks, like crystalized honey, with brows that arched naturally, given him a lively, mischievous appearance.

And his mouth … his mouth was perfect. Wide and teasing, with the slightest permanent slant on the right side. An artifact of the fire, she was sure, but damned if she hadn't wanted to lean in and kiss that quirked up corner on more than one occasion.

He never revealed his right side to her. But every once in a while he would use his left hand to touch her. A firm palm on her back, making her shiver as he steered her along a crowded street. A quick squeeze of her fingers for luck before she went on stage to emcee the Man of the Month contest.

She doubted he was even aware he was doing it, much less the fantasy-filled images those careless touches left with her. That was okay. She was aware enough for the both of them.

Before, she'd always known how to handle a crush. How to either win the guy's attention or move on and get over it. But Griffin was damaged goods, no doubt about it, and Beverly didn't know what to do.

She believed that he was attracted to her too, although that might be ego talking, but even if he were, so what? There could be nothing between them unless he was willing to show her more than just his left side. That, at the very least, was her minimum requirement for getting involved with Griffin—assuming that was even remotely an option.

She hoped it was, because so far, she'd been unable to find the switch to turn off her attraction. The best she could do was try and hide it.

Fortunately, she was an actress, and a good one. She could play the role of devoted friend, of a disinterested girl in a platonic relationship with a boy. She'd been playing those parts with Griffin for months, and now she was ready to move up to leading lady.

So far, she'd gotten no traction on that front.

But the acting life had given her other assets as well. For one, she had a very thick skin and was used to rejection. She was also persistent. No one succeeded in the film business if they gave up easily, and she figured that she could apply that tenaciousness to Griffin, too.

Frowning, she realized that he still hadn't come to the door. The house was small, and he usually answered the door promptly. She rang again. Ten seconds passed, then thirty, and he still hadn't come. She waited a full minute, frowned, then rapped on the door, the hard wood hurting her knuckles.

"Dammit, Griff. Where are you?"

He knew she was coming; he'd even asked for a

head start. But this was ridiculous. Had he stopped on the way to run errands? Or maybe he'd had car trouble? Possible, but not likely. He drove a two-year-old Toyota Corolla, and the car was totally reliable.

She pulled out her phone, then tapped out a text.

Hey, it's me. I guess I beat you to your place. Where are you?

She hoped he say he'd gotten stuck in the Starbucks line, because God knew, neither of them could work without coffee. Except even after five minutes he hadn't told her to wait or to stay because he hadn't responded to her text.

A niggle of worry cut through her, warring with a harsh ribbon of irritation. He knew they needed to work on revisions. They'd said they were going to start now. If he was running late, shouldn't he do her the courtesy of telling her?

And since she had the moral high ground here, she was going to hang out and wait for him.

Just in case, she tried the door, but it was locked, and so she decided to wait on one of the swinging benches in his xeriscaped backyard. She headed down the porch, then followed the little flagstone path to the long driveway that marked the east side of the property.

The house itself stood near the street, with most of its yard in the back. The long driveway followed one side of the house, bordering a section of the backyard and ending at a detached garage that held the washing machine and dryer, all of Griffin's various tools and gadgets, and the classic Mustang on blocks that Griffin was restoring.

As soon as she hit the driveway, she realized she should have gone there first. The garage door was open, and the Mustang was facing forward, its hood open. Griffin's back was to her as he bent over the engine. He wore jeans and a plain white T-shirt. Hanes, she thought. Just like the men's undershirts that she kept around her house for when she cleaned or painted or did other messy chores.

He wore tight jeans, and they hugged his ass and thighs in a way that made her mouth go a little dry. She'd always known that Griffin had a good body— he worked out, and he filled out his clothes just fine —but this view gave her a whole new perspective. A dangerous perspective considering how high he was registering on her lust-meter lately.

She let her gaze wander up, enjoying the broad expanse of his back and shoulders, and—when he reached for something on the far side of the engine —she realized that the shirt had short-sleeves. Which meant that his right arm was completely exposed.

She couldn't see much, he was in shadows, and he was using his arm to hold something while he manipulated something else with a tool in his left hand. Despite the extensive muscle damage and missing pinkie, she knew his fingers worked fine. She'd seen him type on many occasions, although he tended to wear leather gloves that revealed only the tips of his fingers.

The afternoon light filtered across the yard from the west, illuminating the right side of his body so that, even from a distance, she could see the gray, ridged scars that covered the entirety of his damaged arm. Evelyn had told her that his healing process had been more problematic than many victims because he'd suffered a series of reactions that had limited what the burn team had been able to do. Later, he'd been part of a special protocol to help with his range of motion, and while that had offered him some relief, it was hardly a cure.

"I remember he thought about covering the scars with tattoos, but when he tried a small bit of test ink, it didn't go well," Evelyn had said. "More reactions."

"So he's stuck," Beverly had said, and Evelyn had nodded.

"It's who he is," Evelyn had told her. "The only question is how well he comes to terms with that." She'd shrugged. "Personally, I think he's doing a damn fine job."

So did Beverly, actually. In all areas except personal relationships. Unless she was completely misinformed, sex and intimacy were a dead zone for him. And that fact would have broken her heart no matter what. The fact that she longed to be the woman in his arms only made the ache more palpable.

She remained motionless on the driveway, unsure what to do. She knew that he would be angry if he saw her; she was violating his privacy, seeing a secret he wanted to keep hidden. And yet now that she was here she didn't want to leave.

She'd been invited, after all, and she wanted to see this, wanted to know this. Wanted to share his secrets in a way that she could never remember wanting to share with anyone.

The depth of that desire unnerved her, and she told herself that she needed to leave. That he deserved his privacy.

She was about to do that, about to force herself to escape, so as not to embarrass him, when she saw him flinch as if something had blown into his face.

He jumped back, and she heard him snap, "Dammit!" That was followed by another curse she couldn't quite hear, though the tone was clear enough.

And then, without any warning at all, he grabbed the bottom of his shirt and, in one quick motion, he yanked it over his head and tossed it aside.

She saw the black stain as the white material went flying, and realized that somehow he'd been squirted with engine oil. That fascinating fact, however, was incidental to the real spectacle in front of her—Griffin Draper standing bare from the waist up, his jeans slung low on his hips, the cords and planes of muscles on his back sleek and perfect, then twisted and raw on his right side.

The scars rose in twisted ridges, the color almost like Texas granite, mottled shades of black and pink. She didn't know whether this was the result of his reaction to the skin grafts or simply the healing of the burns.

She didn't know, and she supposed it didn't matter. She was seeing the depth and the extent of the horror that had happened to him as a child. She was seeing the suffering that he had lived with for over a decade.

It looked painful, and she knew that it was. Not all the time, maybe, but in weak moments she had seen him shift uncomfortably in his chair, and she'd watched as he went into the kitchen, without mentioning it, to take the pain pills that she had once glimpsed tucked in behind the boxes of Earl Grey tea bags.

Her throat thickened with tears, and she longed to touch him. To run her fingers over the smooth skin on the left, soaking in his strength as she moved on to trace the ridges and pattern on the right.

She wanted those strong, muscled arms to pull her close. And she wanted his right arm wrapped as tightly around her as the left with no hesitation or shame or fear.

But that, she knew, wouldn't happen. She was seeing something he kept hidden. Something forbidden.

Guilt rose within her. She should've eased away sooner. She shouldn't be seeing this. He wouldn't want her to.

Finally spurred into action, she took a step back and heard the crunch of gravel beneath her heel. The sound cut through her like a live wire, and she flinched even before he turned, his eyes first going wide and then narrowing with anger.

"Jesus, Bev! What the hell are you doing here?"

Chapter Three

GRIFFIN'S WORDS slammed against Beverly with all the force of a slap, and she stumbled backward, tears pricking her eyes. "I'm sorry! I was going to wait for you in the backyard because you hadn't answered the door or your text, and I—"

"*Shit.*"

The word wasn't directed at her; that was the only consolation she could take. Instead it was under his breath.

Even so, she didn't wait to see what he said next. Her cheeks flamed, she felt terrible, and she turned and ran back toward the street. Back toward the safety of her car.

Once inside, she tried to start the engine, but her hand shook too badly. She was still trying to get the key into the ignition when she heard the hard tap on the glass and saw his shadow fall over her.

Beverly froze, her fingers tightening on the keys. She didn't want to look left. Didn't want to see him standing there and catch the anger in his eyes. Or, worse, the humiliation that she'd seen something private that he didn't want to share.

She blinked back tears, realizing in a flash of violent awareness, that what hurt the most was not the shame and anger she felt for violating his privacy, but the hard, cold loss that came from knowing that the thing she desired the most was his open willingness to share with her. More, even. She wanted shared secrets. Confessions. She wanted to truly know him, this man with whom she'd spent so much time, and whose imagination she admired so much.

But all she'd done today was hurt him.

Schooling her face into a bland expression, she finally turned. He stood there, as stiff as a statue, then made a twisting motion with his left hand, indicating that she should roll down the window. To do that, she had to start the car, and as soon as she had, she considered simply pulling away and running from this sad, embarrassing, heartbreaking nightmare.

Instead, she pushed the button to make the window descend at the same time as she drew in a breath, intending to let loose with a stream of apologies.

But before she could speak, his words reached her. "Sorry," he said simply, his voice level and even. "I got distracted working on the car and lost track of the time."

"Why were you working on the car?" The moment she asked the question, she wanted to call it back. That was hardly the point.

He lifted a shoulder, and she noticed that the blue t-shirt he was wearing was on inside-out. Presumably he'd grabbed it in a hurry from the dryer. "I wanted —doesn't matter. At any rate, I should have been waiting for you. Should we head in and start tackling revisions?"

For a moment she just sat there. She wanted to tell him that it *did* matter. That he could tell her anything. That she didn't care about his burns.

She wanted to reassure him that not only was everything the same between them, but it could be better if he only wanted it to be.

But all she said was, "Sure."

***

WHAT THE HELL was wrong with him?

He'd known she was coming. Had been perfectly aware that she'd be only an hour behind him.

So what had possessed him to change into work clothes and settle in under the Mustang's hood?

The easy answer was that he'd wanted to work off some of the excitement and stress from the meeting, and so he did what he always did—he'd dived into a project that required working with his hands.

The harder question was why had he still been there when she'd arrived? That answer wasn't nearly as easy. After all, he'd only intended to open the hood, make a few tweaks, then head back inside. He'd told her an hour, after all. But he'd let himself get lost in the machinery. In the beauty of the engine and the way it was put together. He'd lost track of time, and that had been stupid. Careless. And he was never, ever careless. Not even around Megan, with whom he'd become good friends.

They'd hit it off when she'd come into The Fix one day with Reece Walker, who back then had only been a manager, though now he was a co-owner of the place. Reece had needed to take care of a few things—most important the unexpected arrival of his best friend and secret crush, Jenna Montgomery.

Since it had been late, Griffin had offered to walk Megan home, and they'd bonded on the streets of Austin. She was a great girl—now happily in love with Parker Manning—and Griffin counted her among one of his closest friends.

But even she had only gotten a peek here and there at his scars. Why? Because he'd become an expert at protecting himself.

Which begged the question of why he'd been working in the open and wearing short sleeves when he knew damn well that Beverly was coming by.

Had he been testing her? Had he wanted to see if she'd run screaming in horror?

Or had it been all about him? Was his subconscious

intentionally trying to disgust her so that he would once and for all rid himself of the fantasy that maybe somehow, someway, in some magical parallel universe, he could end up with Beverly Martin in his arms?

God, he was a fool.

He turned as she entered the house, her eyes darting away from his the second they connected. He felt that horrible twisting in his belly and wanted to beg her to look at him—to just *look*—and to see him the way no one else did.

But all he said was, "Coffee? Or do you want champagne to celebrate? Which I don't have, but I think I have some white wine chilled."

"I think pretend champagne sounds like a great idea. I—"

"What?"

"Nothing." The word came out fast and clipped, followed by an uncomfortable laugh. "I'm not even sure what I meant to say." Her smile seemed overly bright, and his chest tightened, like a sinking man who needed oxygen but wasn't going to get it.

"Right. Okay, then. I'll be right back."

She nodded, and when he returned, she was settled in her usual chair behind the massive desk that took up most of the far wall of his living room. "So I had a few ideas for the scene where Hammond first sees Angelique," she said. "I love what you've already got, but I have a way to build on it. Can we start there?"

"Sure," he said, then handed her a glass. He was tempted to give her the glass in his right hand, just to watch her reaction. Because damned if he didn't want a reaction. Hell, he expected one. And yet she hadn't said one thing about what had happened outside, although the room seemed filled with unspoken words.

On the contrary, he was certain that she was intentionally avoiding the topic, because when had they ever dived straight into work?

Was she trying to be polite? Or, more likely, was she so disgusted by what she saw that she'd do anything to erase the memory and avoid the conversation?

That probability was the one he feared. The one that had the power to hurt him more deeply than any of the flames that had scarred his body. He'd let her live too long in his fantasies, spinning movies in his head where she was in his arms, her hands touching him, her lips kissing him. Her face revealing only love and not the slightest bit of disgust.

He should never have given in to those thoughts, he knew that. But he couldn't change what he wanted anymore than he could change the skin on his body.

None of it mattered, though. That was the world of fantasy. In reality, she couldn't even look at him. Hadn't this evening proved that? And if the best they could manage was friendship … well, he could live with that. What other choice did he have?

He forced himself to sit in front of the monitor, then tried to control his heartbeat when she rolled her chair up beside him. "Hang on," he said, "and I'll find that section."

"No prob." She licked her lips, another sign that she felt nervous and awkward. Great. She'd seen his skin and everything had gone weird between them.

"Do you want to ride to The Fix with me?" she asked. "You and Megan are probably hanging out afterwards, right? So she could give you a ride back if you don't want to wait for me. I'm going to watch Spencer and Brooke's premiere tonight."

"Sure," he said, his heart sinking a little with the question. She knew he and Megan were friends, and only friends. Everyone at The Fix did. Not only had they tried to be clear about that from the get-go, but as soon as she and Parker became an item, they'd doubled their efforts.

In light of all that, he suspected that Beverly had asked the question as a way to telegraph her desire to jump on the friend wagon, too. Friends—and nothing more.

He exhaled slowly, allowing his fantasies to shift into a more realistic pattern. And then he turned his chair to face her, mentally sprinted forward, and jumped straight into the deep end of the pool anyway.

"You've seen more than she has, you know." He watched her eyes as he spoke, those chocolate brown eyes so wide it seemed as though he could drown in them.

"More?"

"Of my scars."

She blinked, but otherwise her expression didn't

change. "Oh." She swallowed. "I'm sorry about that. I didn't mean to——"

"No," he interrupted. "It's okay." He leaned back, sighing as he tried to wrap his head around his mess of thoughts. "I never—I hate everything about them, you know. Hate the memory of the fire—not that I have much memory. Hate myself for being stupid enough to try to start a grill with gasoline."

She cringed, but didn't say anything, and he pressed on.

"For a while, I hated the doctors. They should have been able to fix me, right?"

Her mouth opened, and she silently said his name. But that was all, and so he continued. "But this is what I've got. This is the best that they could do. Even with an experimental protocol, what you saw was the best that it's possible for me to be."

"You say that like there's something wrong with you."

He cocked his head to the side. "Don't patronize me, Beverly. We know each other too well."

One perfectly groomed eyebrow arched up. "Screw you, Griff. And I say that with tons of affection. But you're an idiot. Yeah, I get that it's hard and people stare. But being different—even being damaged—isn't the same as having something wrong with you. From where I sit, you're pretty damn amazing. I mean, have you read one of your scripts lately?"

And there it was. More proof that they were riding the friendship train. She'd never be interested in him physically. She was all about his three-act structure.

"Yeah, well, my scripts aren't tattooed on my body. Damaged? Hell, yeah, it's damaged. More than most people even realize. Not even Kelsey, because, you know, it's not like I want my sister to see me naked."

Good God, had he actually said that out loud?

From the bright red color on her cheeks, he was going to assume that he had, and that was damned unfortunate. Because although his right hip and side were in pretty bad condition, all of his necessary parts worked just fine, thank you very much.

Not that he told Beverly any of that, though. Because he could only ride the friendship train so far.

"I do get what you're saying," she said, her eyes

hard on his. "It's just that I don't see you the way you do. Not wrong. Not damaged. Just smart and funny and talented."

That tightness was back in his chest, and he quenched it by polishing off the rest of his wine. "I think we need more."

"Maybe we do."

He started to rise.

"Griffin?"

He paused, looking at her.

"Can I—" The question came with an extended hand, and he shook his head, flinching back as if he feared she'd touch without permission. "Oh. I'm sorry."

"It's okay. I'm just not—"

"Ready?"

"Comfortable." Ready suggested there might come a time when it was okay, and he didn't see that happening.

As if she understood his thoughts, she nodded. "Right. Okay." She stood. "Let's go get refills."

They ended up drinking the next round in the kitchen, pairing the lovely Pinot Grigio with the Chips Ahoy cookies he had stashed in his pantry. The conversation drifted to his Mustang, and he was relieved. He wanted to talk to her—loved the way she listened and asked questions and got into it even though cars clearly weren't her thing.

He was enjoying the casual conversation so much that he lost track of time, though he was consoled to realize that she had as well when she jumped up with a sharp, "Oh, hell! I'm going to be late. I was supposed to meet Megan for my make-up five minutes ago." She pulled out her phone. "I'm texting my ETA. Want me to say you're coming, too?"

"Sure."

Her smile bloomed as he stood up. "Good. Because we should be together when we tell everyone the good news about *Hidden Justice*, and I don't want to have to wait for you."

"Fair enough." He stepped closer so he could grab her glass off the table to carry it to the sink. But she reached out, taking his left hand in her right before he'd picked it up, and the shock of the unexpected connection sizzled through him, an electrical storm sparking inside him in all the right places.

"I really am sorry about earlier," she said softly. "But please believe me when I say that nothing I saw bothers me. And most of all, I want you to know how much I love the script and how excited I am that we're moving forward."

It was the right thing to say. A kind thing to say.

It was also the kind of thing a friend would say, and as they headed out the door to her car, Griffin let go the last small hope that something more than friendship might bloom between them.

Chapter Four

"YOU'RE STARING," Megan said, sliding in beside where Griffin was sitting.

"Not staring. Watching."

"Yeah? Well, you're watching Beverly."

"And your point?"

"No point. Just an observation." Her words were bland, but he heard a hint of humor underneath. "So how's it going with you two and the script? You texted that you had good news and revisions. Did you get any work done today?"

"Not much," he said, trying to sound casual as he glanced back toward Beverly, who was inviting yet another contestant to join her on the stage. "We talked a bit. But we didn't have much time. We needed to get here so she could do her emcee thing."

"Hmm."

He turned from Beverly to look at Megan. "*Hmm*," he repeated. "What do you mean by *hmm.*"

"Not a thing. Should I mean something?"

He stared at her a second longer, then turned back to the stage again.

"Okay, fine," she said. "I just want to know that you're okay?"

Once again, he looked at her, trying to keep his expression bland. "Why wouldn't I be?"

"Honestly, I don't know. But I'm getting a vibe from you."

"There is no vibe." He said firmly.

"Oh, trust me, there really is." Her arms were crossed, and her brows were lifted. She looked like a woman prepared to go to the mat to prove to him that there was a vibe. Honestly, all things considered, there probably was. But he didn't intend to share the reason for it with Megan.

As she spoke, Parker Manning approached from behind, then slid his arms around her waist and pulled her close. With one hand he brushed her long dark hair away from her neck and pressed a gentle kiss there before looking up at Griffin and saying, "There better not be a vibe between you and my woman."

Megan laughed, then twisted her head to meet Parker's mouth for a long, deep kiss. When she came up for air, she was grinning. "Only with you," she said, her fingers sliding up to twine in his perfectly trimmed black hair as she pulled him closer, obviously moving in for yet another kiss.

Griffin cleared his throat. "Get a room, you two."

"If you insist," Parker said, the amusement clear in his voice. "There's probably a vacancy down the street at the Driskill. If not, I can give Derek a buzz and see if we can get a suite at the Winston."

"Oh, no," Megan said. "Not even for you am I going to miss Brooke and Spencer's premiere." She glanced at the clock over the bar. "It's about to start in the back. You ready to go?"

"Lead the way," Parker said.

She held his hand and they started in that direction. "You should tell Beverly we're going to watch," she added to Griffin.

"I'm sure she'll hear about it on her own."

"Okay. If you want to risk it."

She started to dance away, obviously amused with herself. He took her elbow and pulled her back. Parker's brow went up. "I need her for a minute," Griffin said.

Parker met his eyes for a second, then nodded. His attention shifted back to Megan. "See you back there," he leaned forward, gave her a quick kiss on the cheek, then headed to the bar in the back.

"You should talk to her."

Griffin fought the urge to roll his eyes. "I like her. I do. But it doesn't matter. This isn't going anywhere."

"Why not?"

"Don't play stupid, Megan. Not you."

"I might be naïve sometimes, but I'm not stupid. You don't give yourself enough credit. Or Beverly for that matter."

Griffin wished that were true. But all he said was, "Go on. Parker's waiting for you. I'm going to get a fresh drink."

She made a face, but continued on, and he hung back, ostensibly waiting to put in an order. In reality, he was watching Beverly as she congratulated Matthew on the stage, then thrust Matthew's hand up in the style of a referee at the conclusion of a boxing match.

As soon as she dropped his arm, Matthew pulled her into a hug, making her laugh and throw her arms around him in congratulations. Griffin watched, and that innocent, celebratory hug sent all kinds of possessive thoughts tumbling through his mind. Then Beverly led Matthew off the stage, essentially handing him over to the feminine hoard waiting for an autograph or a selfie with Mr. October.

He turned away. It was all so ridiculous and campy, and yet he couldn't deny that it was for a good cause, and he was damn proud of all his friends who'd walked that stage, many of whom had been anointed with a Man of the Month title and would soon be appearing in the upcoming Man of the Month calendar.

So, yeah. Campy or not, he'd do it if he could. But who the hell would want his picture?

Don't go there, man. Just don't go there.

Those kinds of thoughts were for his characters, not for himself. He turned away from the stage as he forced himself to remember as much. To practice what he preached and shut down the pity party.

He was about to signal to the bartender, Eric, when a light tap on his left shoulder startled him. He turned around to find Beverly behind him, standing close enough that he could smell the hint of vanilla in her perfume.

Her smile lit up the room, but unlike when she'd been the emcee a few moments before, this smile was meant only for him. "Pretty cool for Matthew, huh? Although I never doubted he'd win. He's definitely got a calendar guy look."

"That he does," Griffin agreed. "He'd be a pretty poor advertisement for his business if he didn't have the abs and pecs to go with it."

She laughed. "You've got a point. Of course, you're not too bad yourself. You forget, I got a nice look at your back and biceps today."

"Beverly..."

She held up a hand. "Don't *Beverly* me." An unfamiliar sharpness colored her voice. "I get it okay? But that doesn't change the fact that you're ripped."

She pressed her hand against his left bicep, then drew her hand up and over the muscled ridges of his shoulder. She started to slide her palm over his shoulder and onto his back, but the action forced her to step closer, so that now they were only inches apart, and he could feel her breath tickling his face.

He took a sharp step backwards, the motion upsetting the barstool beside him. He felt like an idiot, but if she noticed, she didn't show it.

Instead, all she said was, "I know you work out at Matthew's gym. I meet my trainer there twice a week, and I've seen you on more than one occasion."

"You have? I've never seen you."

"I see you coming and going across the gym. And you're always wearing the hoodie with your head down. But I know it's you."

He couldn't believe he'd missed her.

Her dark eyes flashed. "Look, I get why you wouldn't want to stroll shirtless across that stage, but don't stare at me like I'm insane when I say that you've got a nice build, okay? Facts are facts, right? And honestly, isn't that why you're working out?"

That was part of it. The rest was because the exercise was supposed to increase the beneficial effects of the Devinger protocol, an experimental drug trial he'd been part of that was supposed to help his range of motion and repair some of his nerve endings. But that's not what he told her. Instead, he met her eyes and said, "Nah. I only work out so beautiful women will notice me."

She tucked a strand of hair behind her ear, looking more like a shy teenager than a confident movie star. "Are you calling me beautiful?"

He glanced down at the floor, then forced himself to meet her eyes. "Facts are facts."

Her cheeks turned pink, and she flashed that spectacular smile. He reached for her without thinking, his left hand going to her lower back as he led her to the smaller section in the rear of The Fix.

During the Man of the Month contests, this was where the contestants waited for their turn. But the rest of the time, the space was used as a smaller bar. A place where customers could find a bit more quiet, especially if it was a night when a band was playing in the main area. It had a full bar, though smaller than the long, polished oak bar in the main room, and a few scattered tables where folks could gather.

There was also a mounted flat screen television, and tonight all of the chairs had been turned to face it. He saw Brooke and Spencer right away, and Beverly broke away from his touch to hurry forward to say hello. He did the same, hurrying toward them to offer congratulations and waving to the other friends and regulars who'd crowded into the room to support Brooke, Spencer, and The Fix. And, of course, to watch the show.

Several months ago, Brooke had landed a television deal for a program called *The Business Plan*, a six-episode real estate based reality show that highlighted the renovation of a business. The network had required that Spencer be part of the project since he already had a successful track record in reality TV. He agreed, and a series about the renovations at The Fix was born. As well as a romance between Brooke and Spencer.

To add interest to the show, they decided to include snippets from all the Man of the Month contests, which was why even though renovations were complete, the show was still filming, and would wrap up with the Mr. December contest in just over a month.

In the meantime, tonight's premiere featured the The Fix, Mr. January, and Mr. February—Reece and Spencer respectively.

Because the show was a big deal for The Fix, a lot of regulars were packed into the room, not to mention most of the staff. At first glance, Griffin found the massive form of Tyree, a huge black man with kind eyes and a deep voice. Beside him stood his fiancée Eva and their twenty-three year old daughter, Elena. Eva and Tyree were a story book romance. Separated for more than twenty years, they were finally back together, grabbing their happily ever after.

Griffin was thrilled for them, and a little jealous, too. Hell, he was jealous of a lot of folks at the fix, Megan and Parker included. Along with Reece and Jenna and so many other couples. Everyone seemed to be pairing up, and yet he could only stand back and pine.

Even his former intern, Mina, was happily living with her friend-turned-boyfriend, Cameron Reed.

The same Cameron who was now signaling Griff from behind the bar, asking him if he wanted a bourbon.

"You know me too well. Got any of Selma's Bat Bourbon?" Matthew sister, Selma, owned a local distillery, and since bourbon was Griffin's drink of choice, he was one of her best customers.

"You got it." He poured two shots, then slid the glass to Griffin. But it was intercepted by Mina, who flashed a mischievous grin, then ordered Cam to pour another.

"I haven't seen you for a couple of weeks," she said to Griffin. "Where have you been hiding?"

He shot a glance towards Cam. "I think you may be the one who's hiding."

She buffed her nails on her shirt and hummed a bit. "Might be," she admitted. "What can I say? I've got a hot boyfriend."

"Come on, you guys," Megan called, waving the remote for the TV. "It's starting."

Mina grabbed a seat at the bar with Cam standing behind her, but Griff headed toward the empty seat beside Beverly, his heart pounding like a teenager as he walked.

"Hey," she said, leaning toward him. "In a year, this will be us, sitting here about to watch our movie, right?"

A chill ran through him, but whether that was because of the idea of the movie or because of the woman sitting next to him, he didn't know. Fortunately, he didn't have time to worry about that, because the show started, and the room burst into applause as Austin's Sixth Street filled the screen and the camera zoomed in on the entrance of The Fix.

The logo for *The Business Plan* came on, and Griff fell into watching the show. Seeing the way that Brooke and Spencer planned the remodel of The Fix. Watching as they worked together. And noticing the vibrant, palpable attraction that sparked between them on the screen.

He thought of Beverly, working beside him as they revised the script, and as if his imagination had conjured her, suddenly she was there on the screen,

J. KENNER

introducing the contestants for the Mr. January contest. Reece won that month's title, and when the camera pulled in to show him on stage, shirtless and covered with tats, everyone in the room applauded —and then broke into laughter and wolf whistles when the image of him faded out and his beefcake calendar shot replaced it.

"Sexy!" Jenna called, then squealed when he swept her into his arms, bent her back, and kissed her passionately, his hand resting on the baby bump that was now prominent at about six months. Soon, Spencer's win as Mr. February followed, and then the final credits rolled.

"Terrific premier," Tyree said, standing and holding his hand up for attention. "Not only did it show off Brooke and Spencer's talents, but it makes this place look pretty damn good. And since I'm sure I'll have them and their show to thank for another increase in customers starting tomorrow, I'm giving you all a round of drinks right now. On the house!"

"There goes our profit sharing," Brent Sinclair, a co-owner and the head of security for the bar, called from the doorway, setting off a fresh round of laughter.

Beside Tyree, Elena joined in, then shifted her gaze to the floor when Brent winked at her. Griff turned to Beverly, wondering if she'd caught that interchange, and apparently she had, because she lifted her brows and mouthed, *maybe.*

Maybe, indeed.

And that was one more stitch in his ever-increasing tapestry of envy. Because like it or not, he needed to face up to the fact that he wanted to be the guy with the *maybe.*

And no *maybe* about it. Beverly was the woman he wanted.

Too bad he still couldn't make himself believe that he could have her.

She was so much at the forefront of his mind, that he actually jumped when she took his left hadn't and tugged him to his feet. "Hey, everybody! Griffin and I have news, too. Can we share with y'all and join the celebration?"

"You're engaged!" Selma yelled, then immediately said, "What?" when Easton, her boyfriend and a local lawyer, nudged her into silence. "They're together all the time."

Beside Griffin, Beverly's cheeks turned an appealing shade of pink, but she kept her cool and said, "Not that kind of news. This is more in theme with tonight and the show. You want to tell them?" she asked him, but he shook his head. "Fine. Because I'm about to explode with it. Apex Studios bought Griffin's script. We're working on some revisions, and then—unless things go to utter shit, which can totally happen in Hollywood—we'll start filming next year."

"That's amazing!" Jenna bounded forward and wrapped Beverly in a hug. Griffin knew that they hadn't known each other until Beverly applied for the job of emcee, but after spending so many months working together, they'd become good friends.

Everyone else offered their congratulations, too, and the room exploded into excited chatter and well-wishes, especially from Brooke and Spencer. "You've been down this road," Brooke said to Beverly, "but Griff's going to be new to the spotlight."

"I'm just the writer," he said, fighting a sudden, sick feeling in his stomach. "They won't be interested in me. I've hardly done any press for the web series or the podcast except a few written interviews."

Spencer met his eyes. "If this picture is going to be as big as they expect, you'll get some of the shine, too." He frowned slightly, stroking his beard. "You need to be prepared, buddy."

"It's okay," Beverly intervened, once again casually taking his left hand. "It can mostly be avoided. But Spencer's right. There's going to be press. We just need to make sure we have a plan."

"Great. Right. A plan." Griffin forced a smile, trying to act nonchalant. Of course, this had been on the horizon. He knew that. Hell, he should have been planning already.

But he hadn't been. And he couldn't help but resent that the harsh reality of his condition had once again stolen a piece of his joy.

Chapter Five

"YOU HAVE TO SAY YES," Beverly said the moment Griffin opened the door Thursday afternoon.

"I do?" He leaned casually against the doorframe. "Color me nervous."

"Very funny." She reached out, then put her hand on his shoulder to push him back and was gratified to see that he didn't flinch. On the contrary, he followed her lead, stepped back, and let her enter. Of course, she'd pushed against his left shoulder, not his right. But still, she considered it progress.

"So what am I agreeing to? Because I'll tell you right now, skydiving is out of the question."

"Noted." She plunked the massive Louis Vuitton tote bag she used as a purse onto the small table in the entrance hall, then started to rummage around inside. "I know we should dive straight into revisions, but look what I have. *Ta-da!*" she said, as she pulled out a hot-off-the-press DVD of *Crypto Games.* "Movie night?"

"Are you kidding? I've been dying to see it. But it's only two. Should we work first and then watch?"

"Hell, no. I want to see it now. Chris promised he'd send me a copy before I head to LA on Saturday for the premiere, and I just got this. And we can work afterwards. We'll be inspired. I love this movie, but we need to show Chris that we can be even better."

"Sounds good to me. I live to impress Christopher Deaver."

She rolled her eyes and gathered her things, pleased that he was down for this plan. She'd been afraid that he saw their relationship only as work, and even though they'd talked about watching the DVD, she'd wondered if he was going to suggest that they wait until an evening when they could invite a dozen or so friends to join them.

"There's just one hitch," he said. "I have a tiny house."

"I don't take up that much room."

"Yeah, well, in case you hadn't noticed, there's no TV in the living room."

"Oh." She hadn't noticed. "If you don't have a television, that's okay. We can go to my house. Or we can just pop the DVD into your computer."

"Or we can watch it on my sixty-four inch high def television. The one that takes up pretty much an entire wall of my bedroom. Which has no furniture except a bed, a dresser, and two side tables."

She called upon all of her acting skill and managed to not react one tiny bit. "Works for me," she said. And then, because she couldn't resist teasing him. "Just wait until after the movie if you're going to ravage me. I hate getting interrupted during a film."

For the space of an instant, he said nothing, and she feared that she'd put her foot in her mouth, and he was going to conveniently have a forgotten conflict that kept them from watching the film at all, much less on a bed.

But then his lips twitched, and he met her gaze dead-on and said. "No problem. I'll set a timer."

Delighted as much by the quip as by the fact that he was joking about sex, she burst out laughing. "Fabulous. Now come on. Let's get set up. We can have popcorn, right? You don't have some weird no popcorn in bed rule, do you?"

"I wouldn't dream of making my bed a no popcorn zone."

"Good. So, you set up the DVD, and I'll go make it." She'd done it before. Popcorn was her dietary weakness, and sometimes when they were working, she'd crave a batch. Usually without butter, which drove Griffin nuts. Tonight, she'd butter it. Just for him.

"We're ready," he said a few moments later, coming into the kitchen and talking over the loud popping of the old-fashioned popcorn maker with the clear yellow lid that doubled as a bowl. "What do you need me to do?"

"Pass me the butter from the microwave. And then I'm thinking wine. It's not everyday a girl gets a copy of a movie she starred in."

"True that. But will we get any work done later?"

"Possibly, no. Is that a problem?" She tilted her head and propped her hand on her hip.

"We'll make it work," he said, and she forced herself not to do a victory lap around the kitchen island. She had no idea if this was a sign of a growing friendship, if there was romance on his mind, or if he'd simply turned a corner and was super comfortable with her around. Frankly, she didn't care, although she was hoping for romance.

No matter what, it was an improvement.

They gathered up their things, headed into the bedroom, and as soon as they were settled, Griffin pushed the button to play the movie. At first, Beverly was hypersensitive, and not just because he was beside her and she was noticing every move, every shift, every breath. But also because she was on the screen, and she wanted desperately for him to like her work.

Soon enough, though, she became lost in the movie, enjoying both the wine and the popcorn, not to mention the nice little buzz she was getting.

Although she'd read the script, she was fascinated

by how different the experience of watching the movie was from the actual process of filming. Because, of course, movies are almost never filmed in story order. After a few more minutes, she forgot those details, stopped noticing that it was her on screen, and simply fell into the suspense of a well-told story.

She did for a while, anyway.

Then they got to the love scene.

How the hell had she forgotten about the love scene? But there she was, larger than life, her costar David's mouth on her. His hands on her. And although she'd been wearing a tiny thong, the movie was shot in such a way that she truly looked naked. And now she was sitting there next to Griffin, and all she could do was imagine those were his hands. His mouth.

She kept looking straight forward, forcing herself not to glance sideways and see if he was peeking at her from underneath his hood. She doubted he was. There was a still, uncomfortable tension between them, and she had a feeling his eyes were locked forward just as hers were.

For the entirety of the scene, she barely breathed.

Then, when it was over, she slowly relaxed, finally feeling distanced enough from the scene to lose that awkwardness and reach for the popcorn.

His hand was there, too.

Their fingers touched, and she pulled her hand back. "Sorry, I—"

"It's okay, I—" He stopped abruptly, took a breath, and started over. "I'm not a popcorn hog."

She turned to look at him more directly, trying to read from his expression if he was as turned on from the scene as she was. Or, more specifically, from sitting near him while they watched the scene. But once again, she couldn't get a read on him.

Honestly, the man was as good at hiding his emotions as she was.

"This part's really good," she said, nodding to the television, grateful for the train sequence that was about to begin. She didn't lie; the scene was even better than what she'd read in the script, and it was the lead-in to the climax of the movie, so that by the time the final credits rolled, they'd both fallen back against their pillows, limp with relief that the heroes had saved the day.

"That was awesome," he said. And then more softly. "You were awesome."

She'd been told that many times, but for some reason it meant so much more coming from him. She edged toward him, then reached for his left hand. To her shock, he let her take it.

"Thank you," she said, her eyes on his. She leaned forward, wanting to taste his lips, knowing she was pushing, but not caring anymore. She wanted this. And after the last two hours, her body was on fire.

He cleared his throat, then sat up, tugging his hand from hers, then running both his hands down his jean-clad thighs. "Wow. That movie was over two hours."

She fought the urge to curse, wondering if he was intentionally cutting her off, or if he hadn't picked up on her vibe. She decided to go with the latter. Better for her ego.

"We should go work," he said. "Holt will have both our asses if we hold this process up."

Since she couldn't argue with that, she didn't. She just followed him into the living room and, as they always did, she settled into the chair behind him while he fired up the computer.

At first, she felt both awkward and denied. Thankfully, that passed as she got lost in the script.

"This line is redundant," Griffin said, highlighting a block of text. "Hammond said almost the same thing last scene. Ditch it?"

"Absolutely." She leaned forward as he scrolled down, then pushed a strand of hair out of her eyes. "And I don't think Angelique would argue with Hammond right now."

She stood up, one hand on the back of his chair as she reached over to tap the screen. "This bit," she said. "It doesn't quite sound like him."

Her mouth was close to his head, and she breathed in the freshly washed scent of his ever-present hoodie as well as the masculine scent of the man himself.

She eased back, the longing she'd felt on the bed rushing back.

Down girl.

"You may be right," he said, moving the cursor to

highlight some text. "She's not going to show her cards yet."

"Exactly." She started to stand up straight, but stumbled, her balance off a little, probably because of the wine. She steadied herself by resting her hand on his right shoulder. She felt the hard, ridged scar tissue beneath his T-shirt and hoodie. And she also felt his muscles tense.

"Beverly."

"Yes, that line," she said, pretending to misunderstand.

"Beverly, don't."

"Don't what?"

For a moment, he was silent. "You know."

She waited a beat, then another. Then she lifted her hand off his shoulder. But, dammit, this was getting ridiculous. She couldn't be in the same room with him without fighting her way through an electrical storm of attraction, all the more intense because he never let lightning strike. Which was a stupid metaphor, but that only proved how much he was messing with her mind.

And, dammit all, she was desperately turned on.

Time to take a stand.

She moved around his chair, then leaned against the desk so that she was facing him, the computer at her back, and Griffin right in front of her. That close, there was no way she could avoid seeing the massive scars, now illuminated by the glow of his computer screen.

"Beverly." Her name was a growl, and he tilted his head down, putting his face in shadows.

"Dammit, Griff. There's something between us. I felt it, and I know you did, too. So what the hell is wrong with you?"

"Wrong with me?" His head jerked up, his voice filled with anger and derision. "Take a goddamn look."

"I've been looking for months," she retorted. "I don't see a thing."

"Do *not* patronize me."

"You're an idiot. You know that?"

He rolled his chair backwards. "We're done for today."

She grabbed the arms and pulled it back. "No, we're not." She closed her hand over his right one, the rough, destroyed flesh hard beneath her palm.

For a moment, their eyes met, then he looked away.

She took a breath for courage, then lifted her hand, moving it to his hoodie. Gently, she pushed it off his head.

"Don't," he said, his voice tight.

"Then stop me," she said, cupping her palm over his scarred cheek. She met his eyes again, her heart pounding as she waited for him to do just that. And then, when he stayed motionless, she did what she had wanted to do for ages. She bent forward, closed her mouth over his, and kissed him.

Chapter Six

HE FROZE, the competing urges to pull away and to draw her close making him unable to do anything at all. Anything, that is, except to lose himself in that kiss. One beat. Then another. And yet another after that before reality caught up with him, and he pushed her away with a regretful frown and a soft, "I'm sorry."

Mortification bathed her face as she swallowed. "Oh, God. I didn't mean—*shit.*" She drew a breath, and he watched, helpless to ease the awkwardness that had moved in, dulling the electricity that had been sparking between them.

"You know I want to," he continued, "but I can't—"

"Don't even go there," she snapped, embarrassment clearly giving way to anger. "Can't? Goddammit, Griffin, you can do anything you want to with me. And I want you to. Don't you get it? I want you. I want you one hundred percent, and I know you want me, too. So why the hell are you ruining this for both of us?"

"Bev, I—"

But she just shook her head and turned away from him. "I'll—I'll call you tomorrow and we can find a time to work on the script. This was stupid. Tonight was stupid. Tomorrow, I promise, I'll have erased it from my mind."

He believed her. And the sudden realization that this might be his last chance to touch her—*to have her*—cut through him as viciously as a serrated blade.

Her hand was on the doorknob, and he crossed to her in two long steps, grabbing her hand and tugging her toward him.

"Griffin, what—"

But he didn't let her finish. And he damn sure didn't give himself time to change his mind. Instead he cupped her head with his right hand, not feeling the hair that brushed his burnt, damaged skin, but rejoicing in the pressure of her head against his open palm.

And then, before she could utter another syllable, he drew her closer, bent his head, and claimed her mouth with his.

The kiss was slow and deep and colored by the depth of the attraction they'd been battling. But there was no more battle now—there was only surrender.

"Bed," she said, and he picked her up, carrying her like a bride to his bedroom.

"Beverly, I want—hell, I don't want to hurry this, but I want you so bad I'm not sure I can go slow."

"Believe me. Right there with you." She grabbed his sweat jacket and tugged him down onto the bed with her. Her fingers closed on the zipper. "Are you sure?"

He felt a sharp stab of fear, but the look of genuine desire in her eyes calmed him, and he nodded.

She unzipped the jacket, and he shrugged it off, the hood and the sleeves abandoned to nothing more than a short-sleeved T-shirt, so that he was now revealing more than he'd revealed to almost anyone.

Her eyes met his before traveling to his face, his scalp. He knew she was seeing the burn around his eye. The section of his scalp where no hair would grow again. The mottled, raised scars where there should be smooth skin.

Gingerly, her hand went to his brow. "Can you feel this?"

He shook his head. "No. Not anywhere the scars are bad. The nerve endings were destroyed. We thought a drug trial I was on might restore feeling, but it didn't." He shrugged. "It wasn't a total loss, though. I got back some range of motion. You should appreciate that this evening," he added, winking his left eye at her and making her laugh.

"Well, what about here?" she asked, brushing her finger over his left eyebrow.

"That I've got."

"And here?" This time her fingers traced his lips, and when he started to say yes, she slipped her finger inside his mouth, then closed her eyes as he sucked on the digit.

"I like that," she said. She opened her eyes, then hooked her arm around his neck. "And what about this?" she asked then pulled him in for a kiss. But this was no slow, seductive kiss. This was wild. This was passion. This was kissing as sex, and as their mouths moved together, hot and sinful, he felt his cock get even harder than he already was. His body primed. Craving. *Needing.*

"Take off your shirt," she demanded, her voice breathy when they broke the kiss.

"You first," he replied, making her laugh. He didn't give her time to answer. Instead, he began to slowly unbutton the tiny, flower-shaped buttons on her blouse.

"Rip it off," she said.

He looked at her, his brow raised.

She shrugged, looking a little sheepish. "Call it a fantasy. I want you to rip my clothes off."

He laughed, but didn't object, and he grabbed both sides of the blouse, yanked them apart, and sent buttons flying as the pale blue of her lace bra was revealed.

Bending, he tugged the cup down, freeing her

breast. He closed his mouth over the nipple and sucked, gratified when she arched and squirmed under him, begging him for more.

With his left hand, he freed her other breast, then rolled her rock-hard nipple between his fingers. Beneath him, she squirmed and arched, her hips moving beneath him in a rhythm that simulated sex, and made him that much harder—and that much more ready for the real thing.

"Pants," he said, kissing his way down her bare belly, now exposed by the open shirt. When he reached the button of her jeans, he moved his hands from her breasts, then used his left thumb and forefinger to undo the button and zipper. He'd trained his right hand to type, but without nerve endings, he was clumsy at detail work, and now wasn't the time to be fumbling.

Without asking, she lifted her hips, and he pulled the jeans off her, hesitating when he reached her feet, since he had to deal with her damn shoes.

She laughed, obviously recognizing his frustration, and he ended up tugging her jeans off, the ballet flats coming with them. He'd gotten off the bed to do that, and now he stayed there, his hands taking her by the hips and pulling her too him. She cried out with surprise at the violent motion of being tugged down the bed, then with pleasure when he closed his mouth over her panties and teased his finger along the line of material covering her crotch.

She reached down, her fingers twining in his hair, pulling him to her as if she wanted him to suck harder, go deeper. And since that was fine by him, he slipped his fingers under her panties and eased them inside of her.

She was so damn wet he thought he might come right then, and as she arched up, her motions drawing him deeper, he knew that he couldn't last much longer without being inside her.

He also knew that he couldn't be inside her tonight.

"Beverly…"

"Please," she begged. "Please fuck me."

"I can't."

She opened her eyes. "Are you…I mean, I thought the fire didn't—"

"No, that's fine. But I—"

He sat back, and she scooted up the bed, breathing hard and frowning a little. "What is it?" Her eyes widened. "Oh, Griffin. I didn't even think. Are you a virgin?"

"No," he said, and he was pretty sure he saw relief in her eyes. "But I've never—well, you know me. This is the first time I've been like this with a woman."

Her brows furrowed in confusion. "I mean intimate with a woman."

"But you said you're not a virgin."

He lifted a shoulder. "Yeah, well, I paid. Years ago. Right after high school."

"And since then?"

"I've been going it solo."

By all rights, he should be a virgin. He'd never been in an actual relationship, after all. But after high school he'd gotten fed up, then trolled the Internet until he figured out how to hire an escort. It had taken four before he found one who'd take his money—and wasn't *that* great for his ego—but she'd been sweet and not much older than he'd been. He'd hired her five times before he realized that he wanted the reality, and if he couldn't have it ... well, he could take care of things himself.

She considered him, then flashed a playful grin. "Well, then I guess we need to pop your cherry."

"I'm perfectly okay with that plan. But under the circumstances, I'm not a guy who keeps condoms around."

"Ah. Right," she said, then frowned. "I think I might have one in my purse. And if not...well, something to look forward to next time."

He couldn't argue, but he also didn't want to wait. And when he brought her purse to her, he was beyond relieved when she found a condom in her make-up kit. She shrugged, looking a little embarrassed. "Just in case."

"Don't look at me for judgment," he said. "I'm getting the benefit of it."

"True enough." She tossed it to him, then sat up. "Get undressed. And then dressed in that," she said as she pulled off her blouse and the bra that was half-hanging on her. "I want to watch."

He hesitated, because this definitely was a first. But the way she looked at him—as if she wanted nothing more than to feel him inside her, as if she didn't even see the burn scars—was such a turn-on that even putting on the condom made him harder.

"I need you," he said when he was done, his body thrumming with desire and the words more heart-felt than he could ever have imagined. "I need to be inside you right now."

Chapter Seven

I NEED to be inside you right now.

His words echoed through Beverly, voicing her own desire. Her own need. She no longer wanted slow. She wanted fast and hard. She wanted *him*.

"On your back," she demanded, and when he complied, she peeled off her panties, then straddled him, his rough, scarred skin rubbing against the soft flesh of her inner thigh in a way that she found strangely erotic.

She reached down, circling his shaft with her palm, then stroking slowly. "Touch me," she murmured, closing her eyes as she enjoyed the hard length of him in her hand, that sensation soon joined by the thrill of his fingers teasing her pussy as she straddled him.

She was so turned on, and her hips rocked as her body begged for more. He didn't disappoint, and soon she was riding his left fingers, her body bucking as he teased her, stroking her clit and fucking her as she drew him in deeper and deeper.

"More," she begged, her hand moving faster on his cock, her other cupping and teasing his balls.

She thought he would beg her to take him inside her, but he didn't. Not yet. Apparently he was enjoying the slow build as much as she was.

What he did do was move his right hand to her breast, and the knowledge that he would touch her like that—that he would use the injured fingers of that hand to cup and tweak and tease and tug—sent such waves of pleasure through her that she thought she might come right then.

"Now," she whispered, because she wanted to come with him inside her. "I want you inside me now."

"God, yes," he said, as she moved to straddle him, then lowered herself, taking him in even deeper until it felt as if they were one person. She rose up, then down, teasing herself along with him, the sensation all the more delicious when he used his fingers to play with her clit while she rode him.

"Baby," he said, his voice as tight as his cock. "I'm so close."

"I can tell," she said, reaching between their bodies to stroke him as she continued to ride him.

But he'd obviously had enough of that, and with one quick, unexpected move, he flipped them over so that she was on her back and he had her knees up, exposing her to him. He held her tight, the fact that she was so wide open as arousing as the feel of him entering her, deeper and harder and faster until she couldn't take it anymore.

She heard someone begging, then realized it was her. And as he urged her to come on, to come with him, to follow him over, she felt the pressure that had built inside her give way to the force an explosion, and she went over with him ... all the way to the stars, and then safely back to earth in his arms.

BEVERLY STARED at the coffee maker, trying to will it to brew faster. She and Griffin had stayed up way too late last night. Not that she regretted a single moment, but she needed a serious caffeine jolt to get going. Especially if, as she hoped, she'd get to enjoy a repeat performance before the day really got going.

That hope, however, was countered against the fear that Griffin would wake up with morning after regret. Not because they weren't good together—as far as she was concerned, the judges given them a perfect ten—but because he might have lingering fears or insecurities or whatever it was that kept him focusing on his scars and prevented him from believing that any woman would really want him, much less her.

Frustrating as hell, but maybe last night set him straight, and he'd wake up more clued in to the reality. Especially considering reality had her falling fast and hard for the guy.

"Morning, beautiful," Griffin said.

She turned to face him, her already broad smile widening when she saw that he'd come into the kitchen wearing only a pair of boxers and a short-sleeved UCLA T-shirt. No hoodie, no gloves. So maybe she'd truly passed the test.

Her mind drifted back to all the delicious things they did last night. He'd definitely scored an A-plus. And she really hoped he judged her just as highly.

"So how are you?" she asked, adding an extra dose of flirty goodness to her words. "Coffee?" She stood on her toes, reaching up to get one of the larger mugs from the cabinet's top shelf.

"I'll count this morning as one of my better ones," he said, with a hint of a tease in his voice. "Although I really think you should—"

"Please don't say I should go." The words more or less fell from her lips. She should have held them back—the last thing she wanted was to sound needy —but she consoled herself with the fact that they were true. And as far as Griff was concerned, she'd decided to go the route of utmost veracity.

"Go?" He laughed, then slid his arms around her waist. "All I was going to say is that you should put on some underwear if you want to get any work done today."

She swallowed, realizing that she'd tossed on

nothing but his old T-shirt when she'd gotten out of bed. That grab for a mug had probably given him one hell of a view. The thought brought a wicked smile to her lips as she poured him a cup. "Is that all that's on the agenda today? Work?"

He took the mug gratefully. "Got something else in mind?"

"Well, I happen to know you have a pretty comfortable bed."

"Can't argue with that." He put the mug down and took a step toward her, his naturally arched brows enhancing his mischievous expression. "But here's what I want to know," he added, when he was only inches from her.

"What?" The word came out almost like a gasp. Only moments before, her breathing was fine, her heart rate normal. But with every millimeter he came closer, the more she felt his pull. A wild, sensual demand to which she desperately wanted to surrender.

"What are we doing?" He spoke the words softly, but they felt cold and harsh to her.

"What do you mean?" she asked, her heart pounding with trepidation.

"Just what I asked. I want to know what we're doing. What this means." He drew a breath and straightened, and those wonderfully dark eyes and his overnight beard stubble only seemed to underscore the words and the tone.

But she still didn't get the meaning.

"Are we done?" he asked flatly, the idea making her cringe. "Was the point of last night to get it out of our systems? Or is this something we want to repeat?"

She licked her lips. "Yes, please."

"Why?"

Her brows furrowed as she frowned. "What do you mean?"

"I want to know what we have here. Or, at least, what path we're on. Are we fuck buddies?" he asked, the words making her cringe. "Or are we more?"

She looked up, her eyes meeting his, then drew in a shaky breath. "More."

"How much more?" His voice was low. Intense.

"As much as I can get," she said honestly. "I—I think we have something between us. Something real."

She held her breath as he nodded slowly, waiting to hear if he agreed or if he was going to let her down slowly.

"Good," he said, moving closer, then taking her hands in his. "I think so, too."

She exhaled, laughing as she did, the relief so palpable it was almost painful. "Thank God."

"Ditto," he said, and they both laughed even harder. But a moment later, the laughter faded, and they were simply standing there, looking in each other's eyes. He moved toward her, and so gently it brought tears to her eyes, he kissed her.

When they broke apart, she sighed, then looked at the clock. "We slept late."

"And yet we got so little sleep."

She giggled—something very unlike her—but she couldn't disagree. "Have you got eggs? I could make breakfast."

"How about I take you out for lunch? We could go to The Fix. See who's hanging around."

"Oh. We could." She often ate there when she was downtown, but there was a strange edge to his voice that she couldn't dismiss. "Why?"

His wide smile erased all her worries. "Maybe I want to show you off. Or maybe I want to show *us* off."

Her heart about burst in her chest. "In that case, I'll grab my purse."

AT TWO IN THE AFTERNOON, The Fix was almost empty. The bar had recently started opening at eleven so that they could cater to the downtown lunch crowd, but past one, most customers were back in their offices.

Today, when Griffin held the door for Beverly and followed her inside, he saw only a half dozen unfamiliar people at three tables, and then a few familiar faces scattered along the bar.

"Bar or table?" Griffin asked as he took her hand.

"Bar," she said firmly, as he followed her gaze to where Mina was chatting with Cam as he stood behind the bar. At the far end, Brent and Reece huddled over something that looked like a ledger, and behind them, in the doorway, Jenna leaned against the doorjamb with her hand on her belly as she talked with Tyree and his fiancée, Eva.

"Hey, you guys," Cam said in greeting. "You here for working, eating, or both."

"Right now, we're eating and celebrating." He squeezed her hand. Her *left* hand, which meant he was holding her with his right. "Work can come later."

"Celebrating? You mean the script?" Cam chuckled. "Or have you sold something else amazing to Hollywood?"

"Stop it," Mina chided. "Selling a script to a major studio is worth multiple days of—oh!"

Griffin pulled out a chair for Beverly as Cam frowned at Mina.

"Oh? What, oh?" Cam asked, but Mina ignored him, coming over to stand behind Griffin and Beverly.

"Seriously? Oh my God! I'm so happy for you!" She threw her arms around him and hugged, and Griff did his best not to flinch—which wasn't too hard since the contact was all through his hoodie. Besides, this was Mina, his former intern, and he knew her well.

"Seriously, guys," Cam said, clearly baffled as Mina repeated the process by capturing Beverly in a hug as well. "What the hell?"

"You doofus," Mina said. "They're dating."

Cam's confusion shifted into a smile. "Yeah?"

"Yup," Beverly said, and if he'd had any doubts, the pleasure in her voice would have erased them all.

"Wow," he said. "That's great. Drinks on the house."

"Um, hello?" Reece's voice drifted down from the far end of the bar. "Why did I promote you to weekend manager?"

"A good question," Griffin said, "since he seems to be here as much during the week as on the weekend."

"Griff and Beverly are an item," Cam called back.

"I'm supporting this place's growing reputation as an alternative to Internet dating sites."

"No lie," Mina said, as Cam continued. "A lot of folks have hooked up inside these walls." She frowned. "Well, maybe not *inside* the walls…"

Cam smirked. "As for the weekday work, I don't have classes this week, and Eric needed someone to cover for him." He shot a grin toward Reece. "It's my loyalty and commitment to this place that landed me that awesome managerial position."

"True enough," Reece said. "And congrats, you two. How long has this been going on?"

Griffin watched as Beverly's cheeks bloomed pink. "Pretty much since last night," he said.

"It was a hell of a night," she added, leaning over to Mina as the girls laughed together.

"I'm so happy for you both." Mina's whisper was obviously meant for Beverly, but Griffin heard it and he drew in a satisfied breath. Yeah. This was good.

"What are we celebrating?" Tyree's low voice filled the bar as he and Eva headed toward them, followed by Jenna and Brent, who was still scowling at a sheath of papers.

Jenna stepped in beside Reece, and he immediately pulled her in front of him, his hands going protectively over her baby bump.

"Coupledom," Beverly said in response to Tyree's question. She took the glass of bourbon Cam offered her, then lifted it to Griffin's. "To us."

"To all of us," Cam said, pouring a round for all of them. Griff couldn't help but smile. He was right. Cam and Mina. Tyree and Eva. Reece and Jenna. Now him and Beverly.

He frowned, realizing Brent was the odd man out. Brent, however, was too engrossed in his document to notice.

"Yo, Brent." Reece's voice tugged Brent from work. "Grab a glass. We're toasting Griffin and Beverly."

"Oh. Sure." His expression cleared, and he obviously realized the import of the words. "Hey, that's fabulous. Seriously, congrats, you two."

"Thanks," Beverly said, as Reece asked, "What are you looking at, anyway?"

Brent tossed the papers onto the bar. "Trying to get a bead on our graffiti artist. I'm checking the specs and alignment procedure on the damn security cameras. Right now we've got nothing except on number four, and all I can see there is a person, probably male, in dark jeans, a dark sweat jacket, and a dark hood."

"What happened?" Beverly asked.

"Someone pretty much covered the east side of the building with graffiti. And not the artistic kind," Tyree explained, anger lining his usually calm voice.

The Fix was located in an historic Austin building that took up the corner of one block on Sixth Street. Which meant that it had an entrance on Sixth Street, but also a long, limestone wall on the east side that had a few windows and went all the way back to the alley.

"We'll find them and stop them," Eva said, her hand closing over Tyree's arm. "Brent's on it."

"I've had someone spray over the vulgar bits," Brent said. "And Reece has called a contractor to come blast it off. But I want to make sure we have a better plan in place to catch taggers. Bonus points if we can implement something to prevent it."

"Maybe it was a one-off," Beverly suggested.

"I hope so," Brent said. "But I'm planning for the worst."

As he spoke, the front door burst open and Elena hurried in. Tall and slender with a stunning face and short dark hair, Beverly thought that the younger woman could easily be a model. The daughter of Tyree and Eva, she had features from both of them, and the combination was absolutely beautiful.

"What's wrong?" Brent asked, almost simultaneously with Eva.

"I need to talk to you," she said to Tyree. "And to you," she added to Brent, who frowned. "It's about the bar and the historical commission and it's important." Her words spilled out, falling over each other.

"Of course," Brent said, taking her arm as he shot a glance toward Tyree. "We can talk right now," he added, signaling for Jenna and Reece to follow.

Griffin frowned, wondering what was going on. He was about to ask if Cam had a clue when the door opened again, and this time Megan bounded in.

"Is it true? Jenna just sent me a text and—*Oh my God!*"

She glanced between him and Beverly, zeroed in on their clasped hands on the bar, and practically sprinted across the bar. "About damn time," she said, making Beverly laugh.

"I couldn't agree more," she said. "And yet at the same time, my timing sucks."

Griffin frowned, not liking the sound of that. "What do you mean?"

"I have to leave for LA tomorrow first thing tomorrow morning. *Crypto Games* premiere, remember? I'll be stuck there about a week with interviews and publicity and photo ops and all that good stuff. I'm not knocking it—I mean, it's the job, and it's great—but the timing sucks."

"Doesn't have to," Megan said. "Griff's got family in LA. And since he's a writer, he's portable. You should go, too," she added, turning her attention to him.

Beside him, Beverly shifted on her stool, facing him more directly. "That's an amazing idea. Would you? Do you want to? You could even come to the premiere with me," she added, making his pulse kick up and his mouth go dry with horror. "It would be fabulous for you to be my date, and we—"

She swallowed, obviously realizing what she was suggesting. "Actually, just having you in town would be fabulous. The premiere thing was me running off at the mouth, and I wasn't thinking about—"

He pressed his hand over hers, silencing her as relief flooded him. "I'd love to come," he said sincerely. "But I think I'll skip the premiere. After all, I already had a private screening with the star. I can't imagine it would get any better than that."

And then, as much to hide his anxiety as because he wanted to, he leaned over and—with Cam and Mina and Megan watching—he drew her close for a long, slow kiss.

Chapter Eight

GRIFFIN WATCHED as Beverly juggled a series of phone calls as they rode in the limo from the airport to the Stark Century Hotel, a stunning property in the heart of Century City, just minutes from the theater that would be hosting the premiere.

"No," she was saying to the studio publicist, "I can go to the boutique for a fitting, but I need to get dressed and do makeup at my hotel." She paused for a beat as she shot him an *I'm sorry look*, then, "That's fine. Just tell me what time everyone is arriving. Perfect. Great. That gives me plenty of time to meet Chris and get to the press function before we need to do the red carpet routine."

She wrapped up the conversation, then fell back

against the seat, shooting him an apologetic glance as she did so.

"I'm sorry this is so crazy," Beverly said. "Everything moves at the speed of light the day of a premiere, and I made it worse by waiting until the morning of to fly in."

"Not a problem. My sister's done the premiere thing, too." A dancer, Kelsey had made a splash in her now-husband's photography exhibition of erotic images, *A Woman In Mind*. And that had led to a starring role in the film adaptation of a Tony award-winning musical, *The Far Side of Jupiter*.

"Oh, that's right," Beverly said. "I loved her in *Jupiter*. She lives out here, doesn't she?"

"I thought I'd hang out with her while you do your thing tonight." He watched her face, trying to judge if she was truly okay with him not going. He hoped so. He'd been to his share of Hollywood parties—his friend Bird had directed him when he'd done voiceover work for a major release, and Bird had insisted Griffin come to a few parties at his house—but there was no press there, he could dress how he wanted, and he didn't have to stay too long.

A film premiere was basically an excuse to gather

every camera in the greater Los Angeles area in one place.

Right now, he was known as a reclusive writer and voice actor. There'd been some press about the fact that he was a burn victim, but not much, and not in any of the major trades, and it never trended on social media. Griffin Draper had been burned as a child in Santa Barbara. Griffin Blaize mostly remained a mystery.

That, he knew, was partly because his success was small-scale. Success, yes. But not world premier, multi-million dollar movie budget, red-carpet success.

Hidden Justice had that potential, though. And what then?

"We're here," she said as the limo pulled to a stop. She took his hand and offered him a small smile. "You looked a million miles away. Or were you only back in Texas, wishing you hadn't come?"

"Definitely not," he said, lifting her fingers and kissing her hand. "I was thinking that in the not too distant future, we'll have our own premiere."

He thought the words would make her smile, but she only studied his face.

"What?"

"I just—I'm sorry. I was only thinking. I don't want —never mind."

"Beverly…"

"I want that to be fun for you. For both of us." She lifted a shoulder. "That's all."

He started to ask her what she meant, but the driver had come around to open the door. Just as well. To be honest, he understood. She wanted him there, on the red carpet, soaking up the accolades. Not hiding in a hotel like he was doing tonight.

Tonight was her movie, and he'd only be her date, so she got it, even if she'd prefer he came with her. But *Hidden Justice* belonged to them both. If he stayed away that night, would she understand that, too?

It wasn't something he wanted to think about, because that required considering the possibility that he'd make that red carpet promenade, light bulbs popping, recording who he was and what he looked like. And as his stock grew in the industry, they'd dig. There'd be stories on the Internet, pictures on social media. Interviews with the hospital staff at the various burn centers that had treated him.

They'd find out about the protocol and poke into that. And they'd definitely analyze his work to death. Ripping apart his primary theme of physically or emotionally scarred antiheroes who somehow manage to find redemption.

And wouldn't that be fun, living inside a snow globe while the outside world shook him up?

"—don't you think?"

"Sorry, what?"

She flashed an indulgent smile. "I was just saying that this is one of my favorite hotels in the city."

He had to agree, all the more so as they passed through the ornate lobby with the stunning floral arrangements, then finally settled into their penthouse suite, courtesy of the studio.

"This is exceptional," he said, pulling her close as they stood by the window admiring the view that reached all the way to the Pacific. "I should make it a habit of dating movie stars."

"So long as that movie star is me, I have no objection to that policy whatsoever." She spun in his arms and smiled at him. He'd taken off the hoodie once the bellman had dropped their bags, and now he wore only a plain, black T-shirt, his face and neck unprotected.

Gently, she cupped his face, and though he couldn't feel the sensation of her hand against his raw, damaged cheek, he could feel the brush of her thumb along the unburned part of his jaw, and that sweet, subtle sensation shot straight to his cock.

"Careful," he said. "I don't think you have time for more than one kiss."

She flashed a flirty smile. "I didn't realize my touch was so arousing."

"Everything about you turns me on," he said. "How could you not know that?"

"I should," she said, brushing her lips over his, just a quick tease of a promise to come. "After all, I feel exactly the same way." Truth shone in her eyes, and his heart melted a little more.

Gently, she pulled out of his embrace. "I can't

believe I'm saying this, but I have to go. I have a fitting in less than an hour."

"And after that?"

Her delighted laugh filled the room. "Hair and make-up here, and then downstairs to the conference rooms for a series of press interviews. Then back up here to put on my dress. Then it's off to the theater. How about you?"

She'd said it with no bitterness, no question, no underlying hint of disappointment. Even so, he couldn't help but feel as if she was disappointed.

Then again, he was certain that was true. But she was damn good at hiding it.

"You're sure you're good?"

"You forget I used to live out here."

"Right. So you're going to see your sister? Friends? The hotel has an amazing restaurant and bar."

He took her hand. "Seriously, don't worry about me. I already texted Kelsey about getting together, and I promise I'll be here when you get back."

She nodded. "I'm skipping the after-party. We'll have our own."

"I'd like that. But this is your work. Do what you need to do. What you want to do. Enjoy the night, okay. I promise I'm not going anywhere."

Her shoulders dipped as she exhaled, and her words, so heartfelt, almost knocked him over. "Thank God for that."

Her cell phone chimed in time with her words, and she grimaced as she looked down. "Studio publicist. She's got a car downstairs to take me to my fitting." She leaned in to kiss his cheek. "Back soon."

As soon as she'd left, he kicked back to enjoy the room, putting an action movie on the large screen TV, opening a beer from the suite's refrigerator, and settling in to wait for his sister who, in true Kelsey fashion, showed up right in the middle of the final chase scene.

"No talking. No hugs. No catching up. Not until this sequence is over."

She rolled her eyes, but settled in, tucking her legs under her on the couch, and focusing on the film. But the second it was over, she squealed and threw her arms around him. "I've missed you so much. I'm so glad you called this week. Next week we're traveling again."

"You guys need to slow down."

"Nah, we're loving it. We're seeing the world, enjoying each other." From the expression on her face, their *enjoyment* hadn't slowed down at all. "It's great to be able to travel and work together, and Wyatt's new show is amazing. It's like we work during the day, then honeymoon at night."

"Nice." Honestly, he was a little bit jealous. Or, correction, a little bit more. He'd been happy for Kelsey from the moment she and Wyatt got together—well, concerned, then happy. After all, he knew their backstory better than anyone. But it soon became clear that between the two of them it was the real thing. And while he'd been genuinely thrilled for his sister, he'd also felt the sting of envy. Of wishing that it was him who was falling in love and finding that perfect someone.

Now, he'd found her—but while Kelsey and Wyatt were all in, he and Beverly had limits. *His* limits.

"What?" she demanded, because there'd never been a time in his life that Kelsey didn't read him perfectly.

"Honestly? I was just thinking about Beverly."

She adjusted her legs under her as she turned on the couch to face him more directly. "It's serious?"

"It's heading toward serious. I think we both want serious."

"Think?"

"Know," he says. "She wants it as much as I do."

"Good. She seems like a smart woman with great taste. Glad she proved it by falling for my brother."

He rolled his eyes. If nothing else, Kelsey was his biggest cheerleader.

"Tonight's the *Crypto Games* premiere, isn't it?"

"Are you going?" he asked. Kelsey's husband Wyatt was part of a huge Hollywood family and tended to have access to any and all parties and premieres.

"We were invited but turned it down. But I know a lot of folks who are going." She listed a few familiar names from a Who's Who in Hollywood and LA. "We've been on the road so much. But if you're going we could change our plans…"

He shook his head. "I'm staying here. I'm the guy she comes home to."

She put her hands behind her and leaned back. "Seriously? And you just started dating? I thought you liked her."

"Are you kidding? *Like* only scratches the surface."

"Then this is hardly the way to get off to a good start."

"You're one to talk. You and Wyatt got started when he hired you for a series of nude photos."

"Actually, we got started long before that, and you know it. So let's not go there, okay?"

"Dammit, I'm sorry." She was right. She and Wyatt lost touch as teenagers because of him. Because he'd been an idiot with a match.

She exhaled, obviously readjusting her approach. "I get that you're nervous. Uncomfortable. And I don't blame you. But let me ask you this—does she want you there?"

"She understands why I don't want to go."

Her head tilted as she flashed a big sister look. "That wasn't my question. Does. She. Want. You. There?"

He sighed. "Yeah."

"So you're starting your relationship by not being there on what is probably one of the most important nights of her life? Certainly it's her biggest movie by far."

"Kels…"

"Come on, Griff. Are you really going to tell me it doesn't matter to her? Because I bet it does. And you know what? That's a good thing. Caring, I mean. Do you care about her?"

He swallowed, her words making more sense than he wanted them too. "Of course." His shoulders dipped. "I don't want to fuck this up with her."

"Good. Don't."

"But I also don't want to walk down that red carpet and then see pictures of my face all over the trades tomorrow. That's not me, Kelsey. You know it's not."

"I do."

He heard the sympathy in her voice. "And it's not like I can wear a formal hoodie."

A tiny grin tugged at the corner of her mouth. "I

have an idea. What time is she coming back to change?"

"Around six."

She flashed a stage-ready smile. "That should give us just enough time."

Chapter Nine

BEVERLY LOST her smile the second she stepped into the elevator, her cheeks screaming with relief. She'd been on for the last two hours, moving from conference room to conference room as she either spoke to large groups of media reps or did one-on-one interviews with the journalists whom the studio considered influencers.

At this point, all she wanted to do was go into the room, fall face down on the bed, and pass out.

Or, better, strip naked and let Griffin massage her back. She'd learned just how talented his hands were the other night, and she was craving his touch. So much that she'd actually zoned out in one of the interviews, only to be brought back to the present when her co-star had gently kicked her shin under the table.

Now, thank goodness, she had a full fifteen minutes of downtime before the dress would arrive along with the hair dresser and the makeup artist. Somedays, the hoopla that surrounded Beverly The Actress made her feel like a princess. Other days, it exhausted her.

Today, she wished it would all go away so she could veg on the couch with Griffin, watch any movie that she wasn't in, then make love slowly by candlelight.

A nice fantasy, but not one that would happen tonight. Instead, she'd be going stag to her own movie premiere.

She told herself she understood, and she did.

But understanding didn't erase the disappointment. And, yes, the fear. After all, she'd been in the front row as she watched the drama of her parents' marriage disintegrating, torn apart by the distance —both emotional and physical—between them.

Her father had been a long haul pilot, her mother a stay at home mom. Her mother drank too much, and in later years Beverly realized that she drank to forget, or at least to dull the pain of her cheating husband, who, as the cliché went, had a woman in every port.

After her parents' divorce, Beverly's mother had told her that no man was worth losing your heart over. Beverly didn't know if that was true or not, but where Griffin was concerned, she didn't have a choice. She'd fallen so damn hard for him, and she believed that he'd fallen equally hard for her.

According to her mother, though, she and Beverly's father had been head-over-heels when they'd first started out, too. But like erosion, time and distance had chipped away at the foundation of their marriage until it had no choice but to topple and break into a million pieces, too shattered to even try to repair.

Was that what she had to look forward to with Griffin?

No.

It was completely different. He was there for her. Hell, he was just a few floors up. So what if he wasn't coming to the premiere, he was still *there*. Still ready to hold her afterwards, still willing to hear her stories.

But still…

It mattered. She didn't want to tell him the stories, she wanted to live them with him. And yet she couldn't beg. She could only be grateful for what he was able to give. He'd come all the way to LA with her, after all. And that was a lot.

Her thoughts in a jumble, she left the elevator and hurried to the room, hoping for at least a few minutes with him before the insanity of prep began. She slid her key over the magnetic lock, pushed open the heavy door, then stepped inside the well-appointed foyer.

"Bev?"

"It's me," she called. "Are you—"

The question caught in her throat as he stepped into the hallway, and her hand flew to her mouth as she took in what he wore. "Griffin?"

"Does your offer to go with me still stand?"

"Always, but—"

His mouth twitched as he fought a smile. "I couldn't just wear my hoodie. I thought this might do. What do you think?" He turned in a circle, fashion show style, and she felt tears prick her eyes. He'd done this for her. Created an outfit suitable to hide his scars so that she'd have a date for her premiere.

He finished his turn and stood facing her. She studied the elegant silk suit, the raised collar of the suit coat, the black glove that concealed his right hand. She noticed the wig he wore so that it appeared that his hair brushed his shoulders, the right side hanging like a curtain to hide his scars. And the dark gray fedora, the brim tilted to provide additional coverage, along with the dark glasses.

He looked like a character in one of his stories, a wounded vigilante out to save the world. He looked a little ridiculous with the wig and the upturned collar. Mostly, though, he looked amazing. He looked like a man she could love.

"You did this for me?" Her throat was thick with tears.

"For us. It's a little odd, I know. You okay being seen with me?"

She was too overcome to speak, but she nodded, tears staining her cheeks. She brushed them away, laughing as she sniffled. "Good thing someone's coming to do my makeup. You're sure?"

"Unless you've lined up another date."

"Never." She slid into his arms. There was no one else. How could there be? What man would ever give as much of himself to her as Griffin did?

"What changed your mind?" she asked.

"The thought of you. The wisdom of my sister."

"Wisdom?"

"Well, the way she more or less called me an idiot. Rough, but probably wise."

"I can't wait to see her."

"Soon. Right now, I want you to kiss me."

"Perfect timing," she said. "Once Becca gets here to work her magic, there will be no kissing. Can't have smudges."

"So many rules," he said, before kissing her sweetly.

When they broke apart, she playfully tugged a strand of his wig.

"Like it?"

"If it keeps you beside me, I love it."

His expression turned serious. "One thing—I don't

want anyone to know it's me. They'll track me down, start posting pictures. I can't—"

"I get it. That's fine. I'm just glad you're here." She pressed close to him, sighing with pleasure as she felt his heart beating against her. She'd been so worried about the long distance thing, about the parallels to her parents. And here he'd gone and erased those concerns with one fabulous, wonderful, ridiculous costume.

"I'm glad, too," he said. "I couldn't stay here knowing you were there."

"This feels right," she said on a sigh. "More than right." She tilted her head up to look at him, then smiled. "It feels like a damn good omen."

A VELVET ROPE lined both sides of the red carpet leading up to the Pacific Theaters at The Grove in Los Angeles where *Crypto Games* was celebrating its star-studded premiere. Fans and paparazzi lined the barrier, all trying to get a peek or a picture.

Griffin walked toward the inside, Beverly's arm tucked in his.

She looked as beautiful as he'd ever seen her. Her dark hair was piled onto her head, and a thin wire dotted with diamonds had been woven through the curls, making the style sparkle in the light. Her dress was strapless and form-fitting, highlighting her perfect figure, the thigh-high slit accentuating her sensational legs. Her make-up was perfect, giving her the look of a Hollywood beauty from the Golden Age, elegant and coiffed and entirely sophisticated.

It was sexy as hell, and Griffin still couldn't quite believe that this spectacular vision of a woman was on his arm. Even more that she *wanted* to be there.

Now, she held onto him as she waved and blew kisses to the fans. Griffin didn't follow suit; instead, he kept his head down, noticing more about the texture of the carpet than he did about the fans, the surroundings, or the elegant attire of his other companions on the red carpet.

A few fans called out to Beverly, wanting to know who her escort was, but she either ignored the questions or replied that he was her sexy secret. A response that was good for his ego, but made him fear that someone might try to discover the man behind the mystery.

Hoping to forestall that possibility, he kept his attention diverted, almost wishing that she hadn't talked about good omens earlier, because now he was looking for bad ones.

"Doing okay?" she asked as they approached the step and repeat where the actors and other celebrities stood to be photographed, often with their escorts. In this case, Griffin stood back.

As he did, Christopher Deaver stepped in, taking Beverly's arm. "You look positively radiant," the slim, gray-haired man said, drawing her in for a kiss on the cheek. A kiss that had Griffin seeing red. Smoothly, Deaver stepped in beside Beverly, taking a photo with her before leaving her to her solo shot.

When they'd moved off the staging area, Deaver shot a glance toward Griffin. "I suppose I should return you to your escort. Although I swear, if you were solo tonight, I'd steal you away for myself."

"You always know how to flatter a woman," she said. "That's what makes you such a good director."

"And you always know just how to respond. That's what makes you a pleasure to work with." He kissed her hand, then nodded toward Griffin before disappearing inside the theater, for another short reception before the film actually began.

And as he walked away, Griffin felt a cold green ribbon of jealousy curling inside him.

Once they'd entered the lobby, he grabbed a glass of wine for each of them, downed his, then replaced it with another.

She frowned, then leaned close. "Are you okay?"

"Just taking advantage of the refreshments."

She watched him for a moment, and he wanted to call back the words. Hell, he wanted to call back the last half hour. Jealousy wasn't something he was used to, probably because he'd never before believed that he actually had enough of a hold on something that he couldn't lose it. But with her…

God, how quickly he'd come to think of her as his. And seeing her now through another man's eyes only underscored how much he had to lose. And how easy it would be to lose it.

"Oh, look!" A female voice squealed from somewhere behind him. "Isn't that Damien Stark?"

Griffin turned around, then followed the direction

of the woman's gaze. Sure enough, the famous billionaire stood with his beautiful wife, Nikki, just a few yards away. Confident and commanding, the former tennis player turned billionaire CEO of Stark International stood in the crowded lobby looking as if he owned the place. Quite possibly, he did.

"I've met him," Griffin said. "Should we go say hello?"

"I'm thinking no," Beverly said. "Not now."

He turned, frowning, every insecurity rising to the surface. "What is up with you? You didn't introduce me to Deaver. You don't want to talk to Stark. Are you regretting coming with me? Are you regretting letting me out of the hotel in this outfit?"

For a second she only gaped at him. Then she took him by the arm and tugged him all the way across the lobby until they were standing in an alcove leading to the restrooms. Only then, when they had a modicum of privacy, did she lay into him. "What the hell are you talking about?"

"Deaver was all over you, and yet I don't get even a nod? Not as your date, much less as the guy you're dating now. And certainly not as the screenwriter for *Hidden Justice*, because why the hell would he care about that?"

She crossed her arms over her chest, leaned back, and looked down her nose at him with the kind of expression that suggested he was the biggest idiot in the world, and she wasn't sure how to break it to him.

"You idiot," she said, proving him wrong. "Are you seriously standing here and telling me that you wanted me to introduce you to the man who is going to be directing your screenplay right now, like this? And then tell him that he can't share with anyone else who you are or why you're in disguise? I assumed he was a man you'd want to meet as you— in your hoodie, sure, but as *you*."

"I am me," he protested, because jealousy was damn hard to let go of. "You're at a premiere with me."

She stared him down, and he sighed, his shoulders sagging as he gave in. "You're right. I'm sorry. He's obviously got a thing for you. I was jealous."

The corner of her mouth twitched. "Yeah?"

"Maybe."

"Maybe I'm flattered." The smile broadened. "And maybe I didn't want to go see Stark and force you to have to not only explain, but then swear him to secrecy. I mean, honestly, Griffin. This is your charade. Why am I the only one enforcing the rules?"

"Because I'm a jealous idiot?"

Her eyes widened almost imperceptibly, and he watched her, hoping she wouldn't throw her hands up, tell him he was way too much trouble, and then walk away.

She didn't. Instead, she held out her right hand for his left. "Come here," she said, then drew him close. "You have no reason to be jealous." She brushed a soft kiss over his lips, and his pulse kicked into high gear, his cock tightening in a way that made him wish the movie was already over.

"Beverly," he murmured, but she drew him closer, this time using tongue and teeth for a wild, deep kiss, even as she took his left hand and rested it on her bare thigh, exposed from the slit in her skirt.

Slowly, she trailed his hand up until his fingers grazed her sex, barely covered in a tiny thong. He moaned against her mouth, fighting the urge to tease her slick heat, but knowing someone could be watching.

"I'm yours," she murmured as he withdrew his hand. "Don't you understand that I'm yours?"

"I know," he said, her words filling him. Making him strong. "And when we get back to the hotel tonight, I promise I'll take what's mine."

Chapter Ten

"*YES,*" Beverly cried as Griffin thrust inside of her, deeper and deeper, the rhythm of their lovemaking building until her entire being balanced on the precipice. And then, with one final thrust, he sent them both tumbling over, their bodies shattering, the pieces spreading out to join the stars and the moon and the planets.

"Oh, God," she murmured as he collapsed on top of her, and she trailed her fingers idly over the now-familiar rough ridges of his scarred back and shoulder. "Now *that* was the best show of tonight," she said. "Definitely knocks *Crypto* out of the running. And," she added, sliding out from under him so that she could stretch out beside him, "although I loved seeing you in that suit, I definitely like this better."

She reached out again, gently tracing the jagged, discolored line that marked the border between the semi-successful skin grafts on the right side of his torso and the rest of his skin.

She relished these moments when he let her explore his body. Relaxing under her touch even when she traced the burn scars. She wanted the intimacy. Wanted to know him as intimately as she knew herself. And when he let her do this, it filled her heart with the knowledge that they really were on the right path.

"Beverly…"

She bent to kiss him, hiding her smile. At least he'd given her a few cherished moments.

"It's part of who you are, Griffin," she said, honoring his wishes by pulling her hand away, but not willing to back away from the conversation. "This skin, this body. It's been with you since you were twelve. I love the man, Griffin. And the man has always had this cross to bear."

"Love?" His eyes were wide, full of something akin

to wonder, and the full impact of what she'd said struck her.

"I—I didn't mean to say that out loud."

He held her gaze. "But is it true?"

She licked her lips. "I think so. I—yes. It's true. But it's still new. Fragile. And I'm not someone who believes that love solves everything."

She drew a breath, then rolled off him, curling up at his side so she had to tilt her head to see his face.

"In that case, what do you believe?" he asked.

She considered not answering. Saving this conversation for later. Things were moving fast with them, after all. Maybe too fast.

Then again, they'd been friends for months and had spent hours side by side as they worked on the script. She knew what she knew. What she felt.

She only hoped that he felt the same way. "I want to try," she said. "I want to make this work. I think I've wanted that from the first moment I met you. Maybe before. When I saw your heart poured out in your work."

He rolled over to face her, then took her hand and

slowly lifted it to his lips. "I love you, too," he said, his smile spreading slowly, just as hers did.

With a deep sigh of happiness, she moved onto her back, her hand still tight in his. "Can we just stay like this all week? Or do I really have to do all those interviews?"

"I've got your back," he promised. "And every night you've got me in this bed."

Laughing, she turned her head. "I can live with that." She started to roll over when her phone rang. "Hold that thought," she ordered, then sat up and grabbed it off the side table. "Evelyn," she told him. "She probably wants a summary of today since she's stuck in New York."

"Hey," she said after answering. "It went well. I'm sorry you're out of town."

"Then you haven't seen."

Beverly sat up straighter, her brow furrowed as she turned to Griffin. "Seen what?" She raised her brows, silently asking Griffin if he had a clue. He shook his head.

"I'll text it to you," Evelyn said. A second later, Beverly's phone pinged.

She put the call on speaker so she could see the screen.

"Breakfast tomorrow, Bev. We'll talk about how to dodge questions about who your mystery man is."

"Mystery man?" Griff repeated, climbing to his knees so he could see the screen too. Beverly hesitated, then tapped the phone. Immediately, an image filled the screen. Beverly herself, her eyes closed, her expression rapturous. And the back of a costumed Griffin, leaning in for a kiss, the shot taken at just the right angle to show Griffin's hand sliding up her thigh, but thankfully not so high to make the image NSFW.

The headline, of course, was the kicker: *Sexy Plunder. Who is Martin's Masked Marauder?*

And that, she knew, was the question that everyone was going to be asking.

AS FAR AS Griffin was concerned, it hadn't been hard to hang out in the penthouse at the Stark Century Hotel before the premiere. After the photo of him and Beverly started making the rounds, it was even easier to stay hidden away in the room.

Beverly, of course, still had to go out daily for interviews, public appearances, and meetings with various teams from the studio. But Griffin had the luxury of hiding inside, and he was perfectly fine with that.

He worked on the script for *Hidden Justice*. He watched movies. He read books. When Beverly returned in the evenings, he'd go over his changes on the script with her. In turn, she'd entertain him with stories from the day's appearances. And each and every day, she'd have at least one story to share with him that featured some reporter asking her about Griffin.

"You're like a mythical creature to them," she told him one evening in bed. Then she grinned and started to kiss her way down his chest. "Then again, that's pretty much my opinion, too."

Even from the safety of the penthouse, Griffin knew she wasn't exaggerating. When he read an article about the movie on the Internet, the mysterious man at the premiere was mentioned. In the mornings, he'd watch clips from late night television from the night before, and invariably Beverly was fielding the same question. It was ridiculous to him how obsessed the town was about finding out the identity of the mystery man. And he feared that the collective will of the people in the Los Angeles area might end up being enough to put a name to his persona.

More than that, he feared that the fascination might be equally virulent in Austin. Thankfully, that proved not to be the case.

AS PLANNED, they returned to Austin after a week in Los Angeles, and they dove immediately into final revisions on the script, because Beverly would be starting a nationwide press tour on Thursday of the following week.

"I think I want to cut the scene with Hammond and his sister," Griffin said one afternoon when they were working at her house by the lake. They'd gotten a lot done over the last few days, and they'd treated themselves with a change in venue.

Now, they were in her backyard, and he was lying in a hammock with his laptop on his stomach while Beverly edited a printout of that day's work at a nearby picnic table. Or, at least, that's what she was supposed to be doing. Instead, her mind was elsewhere.

"Bev? Earth to Bev."

Startled, she looked up at him. "What? Sorry."

"Where are you? I'm thinking it's not with Angelique and Hammond."

"Sorry, I—nothing."

He sat up, the put the computer on the small table beside the hammock. "What?"

She drew a deep breath and decided what the hell —the worst he could do was say no. "I don't want to leave. Not now." She was scheduled to hit the road on Thursday, right after she finished emceeing for the Man of the Month Contest.

"Because of the script?"

She rolled her eyes. "Because of us."

"Oh." He grinned. "Is it bad that I like hearing that? Because I don't want you to leave either."

"Then come with me. You can record the podcast on the road. We can write on the road. It's a whole month, and I don't want to be apart. So why don't you just come with me."

For a moment, he simply stared at her. Then a slow smile touched his lips. "I like the sound of that. But if I'm with you, we're going to end up dealing with the mystery man bullshit all over again. And we haven't seen much of that since we've been in Austin."

She shrugged. "I'm good with spending most of our free time in the hotel. And it's not like the press in Idaho or St. Louis is going to be following me around. So long as we don't announce where we're going, we can grab dinners out, the whole thing. No way will any of the places on the junket be as crazy about the mystery of who I'm seeing as folks in LA. No one in the rest of the country cares."

"I'm not sure about that," he said. "But I'll agree they care less. And they're a lot less crazed."

"Exactly. And if anyone asks who you are, I'll just say what I've been saying—that a girl has to have some secrets."

"And it is a way to not hold up the script. The studio's going to have one more round of revisions," he said. "They always do. This way we wouldn't have to work by phone."

"See how brilliant I am?" she asked, coming to him. She climbed into the hammock with him, careful not to send them both tumbling. He curled his arm around her and she snuggled close. "I don't want to go away. Not when we're so new."

"New doesn't mean fragile."

"I hope not. Because I don't want what's between us to break."

He kissed her forehead. "We won't. I promise."

Chapter Eleven

"YOU WERE serious when you said there'd be no work today," Beverly said as they walked hand-in-hand down Congress Avenue. They'd just finished a fabulous brunch at the Four Seasons, and now Griffin was leading her somewhere else. He just hadn't told her where.

"I'm glad you told me to wear flats. Are we walking all the way to Dallas?"

"Funny," he said, though she thought the question was reasonable. Brunch had been near the river, which was essentially on Second Street, though it was now called Cesar Chavez. They'd been walking perpendicular to the river, and now they were approaching Sixth Street.

"Are we going to The Fix?" she asked.

"No. Wait and see."

She didn't have long to wait. Griffin soon drew them to a stop in front of Austin's historic Paramount Theater, a beautiful venue that had celebrated its centennial just a few years before.

"What's going on here? Is there a show?"

"We've been working so hard on our movie, I thought we should go watch a couple of classics. Okay?"

She turned to him with genuine pleasure. "Are you kidding? I love classic movies. What's playing?"

"Double feature. *The Maltese Falcon* and *The Big Sleep*. You up for it?"

"Do we get popcorn?"

"Popcorn, wine, whatever you want."

She grinned, absolutely delighted with his plan for the afternoon. "I am totally in."

"Good. And after the movies, I have one other place I want to take you."

"Where?"

"It's a secret."

They got their tickets, hit the concession stand, then grabbed a couple of middle seats, which as far as Beverly was concerned, were the best seats in the house. Griffin had timed brunch and the walk perfectly, so they only had to wait a few minutes before the trailers began.

Beverly munched her popcorn, her hand occasionally brushing Griffin's, the contact sending nice little frissons of pleasure coursing through her. By the time the first movie began, they were halfway through the bucket. He put it on the floor, then took her hand. He lifted it and kissed it gently, then flashed her a quick smile. "Buttery goodness."

She laughed, then leaned in for an even more buttery kiss.

She'd seen both movies before, but it had been years, and she became quickly absorbed in the film noir storyline. So much so, that when the intermission between the movies came, she had a hard time believing that they were halfway through the afternoon already.

By the time the second movie ended, she wished there were even more on the program.

"Did you like?" he asked as they left the theater.

"Are you kidding? They were great. That's what I want to do," she added as they headed back toward the Four Seasons and his car. "Make movies that last. Movies that have that kind of resonance." She paused on the sidewalk, catching his eyes. "Do you think ours will have even close to the merit of those films?"

"I don't know," he admitted. "But I want that, too. The script is solid, and Deaver's talented."

"Now he's talented?" she teased.

"Since you swear he doesn't have designs on you, yes. He went from asshole to filmic genius."

"Maybe we should—"

But she didn't get to finish the thought because he pulled her to a stop with a sharp, "Dammit."

"What?" she asked, watching as he bent his face and pulled his hoodie more forward. Then she saw the answer. There, across the street and standing by the local landmark sculpture of a woman shooting a cannon, was a burly photographer with a long lens, doing his own kind of shooting. And his camera was aimed right at Griffin.

"SO WHERE ARE WE GOING NOW?" she asked, after they'd been driving in silence for at least ten minutes. She knew that he was upset about the photographer, but as she'd pointed out on their walk back to the car, it may have only seemed as if the lens was aimed at her and Griffin. Maybe the guy had been photographing the historic facades along Congress Avenue.

"I don't think so," he'd said in response to that suggestion. And since then, he hadn't said another word.

"Griffin," she pressed. "Either talk to me or take me home."

His hands tightened on the steering wheel, and for a second she feared he'd take her up on the second option. But then he relaxed. "I'm sorry. I know you're right. It might just be coincidence. But I've managed to live my life without being tossed into the spotlight, and I don't really want to go there now."

"I know."

They reached a red light, and he turned to face her.

"I know you think I should just say screw it and stop wearing the gloves and the hoodies. And I know," he continued before she could jump in, "that my scars don't bother you."

"They don't," she whispered, and he reached for her hand, the leather of his glove cool against her skin.

"I believe you. But even then, it was my choice to show you. And those damn social media whores are trying to take that away from me."

"They don't know about the scars. They just want to unmask my mysterious man."

"Same difference as far as I'm concerned," he said.

"I know." She waited for him to respond, and when he didn't, she turned to look at him. His hands were tight on the wheel again, and he was focusing intently on the traffic. Too intently, it seemed. "Griff?"

He drew an audible breath, then spoke without looking at her. "There's one place I never wear the hoodie or the gloves." He turned to her. "That's where I'm taking you."

She started to ask where, but realized he would tell

her when he was ready. So she simply nodded and sat in silence as he maneuvered past the University and then down Red River to Dell Seton Medical Center, Austin's still-new teaching hospital.

He parked in a visitor slot, then raised a shoulder in a shrug. "We're here."

She followed him inside without question, unsure of where they were going until she saw the signs for the burn unit. "You volunteer here?"

"Sort of. I talk to the patients. I try to come regularly, and I always come when they call to tell me a kid's been admitted."

"I—" She broke off, unable to speak through the tears clogging her throat.

"It's not hero shit. I just want them to know that they'll find a way to survive even with the scars."

She nodded, realizing as she did that he'd done that. Maybe she wished he were more open, more out there. But he'd done what he said—he'd found a way to survive. And he'd found a way to let her into his life. Which under the circumstances was pretty damn impressive.

They'd reached the double doors that led into the

burn center, and he tugged off his hoodie, then pulled off his gloves, shoving them in his pocket. "Ready?" he asked, then pushed the intercom when she nodded.

A nurse responded, and as soon as he identified himself, the doors opened. Obviously, he'd meant what he said when he told her he came regularly.

"Just two on the floor today," a nurse with a nametag identifying her as Angie said. "Jessie and an infant."

"A baby." The sadness and horror in his voice mirrored her own emotions.

"He's stable, but in a sterile environment."

"Parents here?"

"They were," Angie said. "They're in a consult with the surgical team right now."

Griffin nodded. "Give them my number. Tell them they can call me if they have questions or just need to vent." He glanced around. "Jessie awake?"

"She's in the playroom."

He gestured to Beverly and they started walking deeper into the unit. "This is a good day. I've never seen the unit with less than five patients, usually more."

"Who's Jessie?"

"She's like me. Her body keeps rejecting the treatments. So she's been in and out for months. She was trapped in a house fire. Arson. Her father. He's in jail. Mom's getting counseling. At first, Jessie was a wreck. Now she says the burns were the price of getting her and her mom free of the asshole. She's fifteen, by the way. Older, though. The stuff she's been through ages you."

"I guess so."

"This center only handles burns covering up to thirty percent of the body. More, and they get sent somewhere else, usually San Antonio. Jessie's just under the limit. Her arm, the side of her face, part of her torso. She's great. You'll like her."

They'd reached the playroom, a large, glassed-in open area with toys designed mostly for toddlers. There was an easel with a pad of large drawing paper, like the kind used in corporate meetings. A tall, slim girl stood there in hospital scrubs sketching, her dark curly hair pinned up—except for the red, raw area of her scalp where no hair grew.

From where she stood, Beverly could see the violent scarring on her neck that presumably descended beneath the scrub shirt. And when Griffin stepped into the room and she turned, Beverly had to force herself not to flinch in sympathy and sadness. The burns covered a pattern similar to Griffin's, though more of Jessie's mouth was impacted. A sad fact that affected her speech, Beverly realized, when the girl turned to Griffin and slurred her cry of, "You're here!"

"Hey, Jess. I want you to meet my girlfriend, Beverly."

Jess's eyes went wide. "I know you! I saw you in *Suburban Love Story*. You're amazing!"

Beverly laughed. "Thanks. That's really nice of you to say." She nodded at the drawing—a portrait of Jessie, but without the burns. "I'd say you're pretty amazing, too. That's an incredible drawing."

"Too bad life really doesn't imitate art, huh?"

"You're still pretty, Jess," Griffin said. "Don't let it beat you down."

She rolled her eyes. "Pretty on the inside, you mean."

"And the outside. I mean, hell. Who decided what pretty was? I say we make up our own definition."

Jess shot a glance toward Beverly. "He's so freaking Pollyanna," she said, and Beverly had to hold her tongue as she shot Griff a questioning look. He was saying to Jess the things she said to him.

Griffin, probably wisely, averted his eyes.

It quickly became clear that the two knew each other well and they caught up on the news of her treatments, her mother's adjustment, and what was in store next. Soon Beverly joined in and they moved on to fashion and movies and boys.

"I got into the Devinger protocol," Jessie said to Griffin after they'd been chatting for a while. "Thanks for writing the letter."

"No problem. You need anything else?"

"Just luck. Another skin graft scheduled for tomorrow. They're hoping it'll take better. My boob," she added to Beverly with an eyeball roll, and Beverly was once again amazed by the kid's attitude.

"Sending you lots of that," Beverly said. "I'm glad to have met you, Jessie."

"Yeah, me too. And thanks in advance for the picture and the DVD. You won't forget? And you'll sign them?"

"I won't forget," she promised, then held her smile until they were out of the room and safely in the elevator.

Then she stopped fighting and let the tears flow. "She's got such a great attitude," she said, when she could force words past the lump in her throat.

"She does," Griffin agreed. "Now, anyway. When I met her five months ago, she hardly talked."

Beverly paused, staying on the elevator despite the now-open door. "That's because of you. You told her all the right things."

"I wanted to help."

"You told her the truth, you know," she said gently. "I mean, one day maybe you should take a mirror with you."

"Beverly…"

She shrugged and said no more. But she'd planted the seed. Because deep inside, he obviously realized that the way to really move forward was to quit hiding. He just needed to practice what he preached.

"Any chance there's ice cream in our future?" he asked. "There's an Amy's Ice Cream not too far away."

"I'm always down for Mexican Vanilla," she said as her phone chimed to signal a text. She pulled it out of her purse and glanced at it as they walked, then came to a dead stop.

"It's from Evelyn," she told him. "She says, *Sorry.* And there's an attachment."

Their eyes met.

"Open it," he said.

She hesitated, then did as he asked.

And there it was, a screenshot from Twitter. The image of her and Griffin on the sidewalk near the Paramount. And underneath it, the words: *Martin's Mystery Man Identified: Griffin Blaize. Podcaster. Screenwriter. Fourth-degree Burn Survivor.*

Chapter Twelve

THE STORY EXPLODED.

By noon on Tuesday, that first photo of Griffin and Beverly on Congress was everywhere, along with the one of him in disguise at the premiere.

That would have been bad enough, but every social media hound in the world had started digging into his past. Fortunately, he'd bought his house in the name of his business trust, so he didn't have a horde of cameramen camped outside, but that didn't mean they hadn't found out about him. Someone managed to prove that Griffin Blaize was Griffin Draper, and had dredged up news coverage of the fire when he was just shy of thirteen. Someone even found a picture from when he was in the hospital.

His career was splashed all over the Internet. Kelsey and Wyatt were dragged into it, and Griffin kept sending his sister apologetic emails, despite her telling him not to worry about it, she had his back, and the so-called reporters were assholes.

He agreed, but that didn't help.

The worst was that he was essentially trapped in his house. He couldn't even go to The Fix, because Megan had told him that photographers were all over downtown, and they were especially thick around the bar. "Probably because Beverly is the emcee. I don't think they know you hang out here, but they do know that you're with her, so it's a good bet."

Which meant he was stuck inside, Beverly with him. But he was quiet and moody. He hated that he was, and hated that he cared so damn much. Hated the scars. Hated wanting to hide them. Hated knowing that he was now the center of a media shit storm, and that everywhere he went, reporters were going to try to get a picture.

He looked at Beverly, curled up on his couch with a red pen going over their pages. They were in the final throes. The Man of the Month contest was tomorrow night, and Thursday they left for the tour. And Griffin knew damn well that the mystery would leave Austin. It would follow Beverly.

Without a mystery man on her arm, it would die down.

His stomach twisted. He hated himself, but he knew what he had to do.

"Hey." He cleared his throat, then tried again. "Bev?"

She looked up, her smile bright but sympathetic. "You okay? The hoopla will die down, you know."

"I know." He swallowed. "I know how to make it die down faster."

She sat up, her brow furrowed. "You do?"

"I'm not going with you on the press tour. Without a mystery guy beside you, they'll get bored."

She blinked. "Wait. What?"

"You're the attraction, not me. The fascination is that you're dating a mystery guy. Probably this scarred writer named Griffin. But if that mystery guy isn't beside you, he's not interesting. So the press will forget it and move on."

"You're not coming with me? I'm going to be gone for a month. Six weeks, actually."

"We'll talk every day."

She sat back, staring at him. "And what about the next time?"

"The next time?"

"When the film opens in Europe, I'll be touring over there. Will you come with me?"

He swallowed. "That would stir it all up again."

She nodded, her throat moving and her eyes unnaturally wide. "And let's say this thing between us sticks—"

"I want it to," he said firmly.

"—and I end up filming a movie in Vancouver. Or a TV show. And I'm there for months. Maybe years. What then?"

He said nothing. By her side, he was a target. Here, he could stay quietly out of the spotlight.

"I see."

"Lots of people have long distance relationships. And you aren't away forever. Even if you were filming out of town, there are weekend flights."

"And wouldn't that be fun?" She licked her lips. "My parents did that. It wasn't pretty."

"We're not your parents."

"No," she said, her voice a whisper. "We're not. I thought we were so much more."

Before he had a chance to respond, she stood. "I'm sorry, Griffin." Her voice was unnaturally stiff, her skin pale. "I love you—God, I love you. And I can't believe I'm saying this. But this is my line in the sand. Maybe you're right. Maybe it would work just fine. But I don't care. That's not what I want—I want the man I love to be beside me. Miss a few trips, sure. But as a lifestyle? No. And I can't—"

Her voice broke on a sob. "I can't start a relationship knowing that we don't have the same vision, and that the life I dream of can't ever happen."

She started toward the door, and panic bubbled inside him. "Bev, wait." He hurried after her. "We can make this work."

"No," she said, "*we* can't. But you can. And,

dammit Griffin, if you want me—if you want *us*—you know exactly what you have to do."

Chapter Thirteen

BEVERLY SPENT the rest of Tuesday and all of Wednesday morning trolling the Internet. She started out cursing every single photographer, reporter, and Internet gossip who posted anything about her mystery man or Griffin or her love life at all. What business was it of theirs, and how the hell could they justify what they did, knowing that it would undoubtedly mess up peoples' lives?

That pity party lasted until Tuesday evening. Then she moved on to the main event—*Griffin*. Specifically, her irritation, her anger, and her hurt because of him.

Because at the end of the day, it wasn't the reporters' fault. Or not entirely. Because if Griffin could just own the fact that he was scarred and step out into the world, then they could be together. For that matter, reporters might actually treat them kindly. And even if they were nasty, it would die down soon enough. Give the press nowhere to go, and they went nowhere.

But to do that, he had to put himself on the line first. And Griffin wasn't prepared to do that. Despite everything he'd said to Jessie—despite the fact that she knew he truly believed it—he still couldn't get past his own fears and insecurities.

And neither could she.

She wouldn't risk a long distance relationship. She was too afraid it would break down. But notwithstanding that fear, she didn't want to spend that much time away from the man she loved.

And that was the trouble.

She loved him. She was certain of it.

And she was terrified that she'd never find that kind of love again. That she'd never find another Griffin.

But, dammit, she wasn't going to settle. She wanted it all or nothing.

She just hoped that at the end of the day, it wasn't nothing she was left holding onto.

GRIFFIN WANTED to kick his own ass.

She was his—or she had been. And he'd lost her because he was too damn scared—and too damn scarred.

But, dammit, he didn't want to live the life she did. He didn't want to be in the spotlight. If he was an average guy, he could probably avoid it, even with a celebrity at his side. But he had two strikes against him—he was already a player in Hollywood and his scars gave him story appeal for all those damn reporters.

How the hell was he supposed to live like that? Like some ugly bug that a kid picked up to examine under a microscope? With the press wondering why a beautiful girl like Beverly would be with a guy like him?

The thought made his stomach twist.

The trouble was, the thought of not being with her made his stomach twist more.

He didn't know what to do, and so he finished off a bottle of bourbon and watched bad action movies on late night cable. It wasn't a cure, but it was an anesthetic, and he was grateful to dull his pain.

The sharp ring of his phone woke him the next morning, and he blinked at the sun streaming in through the windows. He snatched it up, certain it would be Beverly.

It wasn't. It was Jessie.

"So what's your damage?" she said, without preamble.

"Excuse me?"

"Oh, come on. Do you think I spend all my time painting? I'm mostly on my phone. And now that Beverly's my new best friend, I went poking around for her."

He cringed, certain he knew where this was going.

"You're all over social media these days, you know that, right?"

"Yeah. I noticed that."

She snorted. "So, I repeat. What's your damage? Because, seriously? A wig? And a hat? I mean, I listen to your podcast and you sort of look like you might be one of the characters, but I don't think that was the point, was it?"

He had to bite back a smile. Which, under the circumstances, felt pretty good.

"I knew the photographers were going to be everywhere. I wanted to protect my privacy."

"Well, that's a bunch of crap."

A flare of anger sparked in him. "What the hell, Jessie?"

"Don't even," she snapped, and he heard the mirror of his anger in her tone. "I trusted you. I believed you. I mean, what the hell, Griffin? You come in here all rah-rah and tell us that these horrible, ugly, nasty scars aren't going to ruin our lives, and then you go and hide? Who does that?"

He said nothing. She was right, of course. Who did that?

He did, apparently.

"Hello? Oh, come on. Did you hang up on me? That's just the most asshole thing—"

"I'm here."

"Well?"

"You're right."

Silence filled the line.

"Jessie?"

"What did you say?"

"I said you're right."

"Wow. Grown-ups never say that."

"Well, I've been acting like a child, so maybe that's why I can say it."

At that, she laughed outright.

"Glad I'm amusing you. But yeah, you're right, and Beverly is right, and I'm a damn chicken." And wasn't that the truth?

He drew in a breath, then continued. "But I want you to know that everything I told you was true. And I believe every word."

"So get off your ass and do something. Flip those reporters the bird. Take off that freaky costume. And a hoodie? Seriously? Show them the real you."

He bit back a smile. "If I do it, will you?"

"I've been doing it, remember? You're the one who told me to. I've been walking the walk, Griff. You've only been talking the talk. Honestly, man, you can do better."

"Yeah," he said. "You're right."

"Well, duh."

He laughed outright. "Hey, Jessie. Thanks. I needed this."

"Anytime," she said. "And just so you know, I'm going to be stalking you and Beverly online. I'll know if you chicken out."

"Not a problem." He knew what he wanted, and Jessie had just kicked his ass hard enough to make him go after it. "I think I'm about to make you proud."

BEVERLY'S HEAD snapped up as Jenna called her name. "What?"

"I said we're about to start. You okay?"

"Yeah. Sorry. Griff and I—doesn't matter." She was a professional. She had a job to do. She could pine over her lost love after she did her emcee routine.

A small smile tugged at Jenna's mouth. It looked like amusement, but Beverly was certain it must be sympathy.

"All the guys are in the back and the reality show cameras are running. The contestant cards are on the podium, and I'm going to cue your music, okay? You're good?"

Bev nodded, pulling herself together. Of course she could do this.

She climbed the stairs to the stage, looked out at the crowd, and allowed herself one second to mourn the fact that Griffin wasn't out there watching her. Then she slid into her professional persona, ran through her usual spiel welcoming everyone to the contest, and glanced at the first card in the stack that Jenna had left for her. One card for each contestant, it had general information about the men so that she could properly introduce them to the waiting crowd.

After having done this so often, she could do it in her sleep. But she never did. The truth was, she enjoyed the gig. Liked having the audience. And believed in the original reason for the contest—to raise money to keep The Fix going. Now, the contest had become almost an iconic event, and she was proud to be part of it.

Tonight, though, her mind kept wandering, and twice she stumbled over a contestant's name.

She was relieved when she was down to the final two cards, and she watched as the penultimate contestant climbed the stairs, tugged off his shirt, and flexed some pretty impressive muscles. There wasn't a requirement they strip, but of course most of them at least took off their shirt. They wanted to be in the calendar, after all. And good abs got votes.

Unlike four of his predecessors, this candidate didn't make a speech—apparently he thought his impressive build spoke for itself. And so Beverly led the applause as he exited the stage.

She took the final card from the podium, read the name, and almost dropped the paper.

"Sorry," she said, then took a sip of water before plastering on her show-ready smile. "Tonight's final contestant is Griffin Draper."

She heard the low rumble of surprise—many in the

audience were regulars, who knew enough to know what Griffin kept hidden beneath his clothes and hood.

She glanced down at the card, then felt tears prick her eyes as she read the information, while Griffin walked the red carpet. "In his early thirties, Mr. Draper is the writer and creator of a popular podcast and web series, as well as the screenwriter for *Hidden Justice*, soon to be a major motion picture staring—well, it says Beverly Martin, but that's your truly."

She brushed away a tear as Griffin climbed the stairs. He wore a T-shirt. A plain white Hanes T-shirt, and she had to blink to see the words swimming in front of her.

"Mr. Draper recently made the wrong relationship decision because he was too scared to—*dammit*, Griff, how am I supposed to read this?"

The crowd fell absolutely silent as he moved to her side and took the microphone from her. "He was too scared to show himself to the world, even for the woman he loves. But he's not any more." He handed her the microphone, then slowly peeled off his shirt, revealing all of this scars except the ones on his hip and thigh.

Only the sound of breathing could be heard in the room. Not even the rustle of clothes.

"Sorry folks," Griffin said, breaking the spell. "Shirt only. Buy the calendar if you want more."

Nervous laughter exploded into the still air, then changed into the laughter of genuine amusement. He smiled, then moved to Beverly's side and took the microphone again, holding it low enough that he wasn't talking directly into it, but close enough that it still projected his voice. "I love you," he said. "And I'm coming with you."

It wasn't a question, and she nodded happily as applause and cheers nearly blew the roof off the place.

Fifteen minutes later, they were still surrounded by well-wishers and folks trying to get close enough for a picture. Griffin had his shirt back on, but not his hoodie, and Beverly was so damn proud of him.

"You doing okay?" she whispered.

"It's freaky, but it's okay. I think I'll get used to it. Eventually."

Jenna bounded up the stairs grinning broadly. "Congratulations," she said. "The vote confirmed what we all knew. You're Mr. November."

"I'm so proud of you," Beverly said, holding tight to his hand.

"Yeah, well, don't be too proud. I'm still going to tell Eva I want her to edit out the scars on my calendar photo," he said, referring to the Man of the Month beefcake calendar in which he would now be featured as Mr. November. "I'm not quite *that* ready to reveal everything."

"I can live with that," she said, laughing as she pulled him close. "So long as I have you."

"You do," he said. And as the crowd around them went wild once more, he drew her close and kissed her hard, just to seal the deal.

Epilogue

"I THINK SHE'S FINALLY ASLEEP," Elena said, coming into Brent's oven-warmed kitchen and taking the glass of wine he offered her.

He'd never seen her look frazzled before. Now her short hair was mussed and her makeup smudged. He'd thought she was beautiful before, but now she looked approachable, too. And he wasn't sure that was a good thing.

"I'm really sorry she wasn't asleep when you got home," she added. "She wanted to watch another cartoon, and we picked *The Incredibles*, and I think it just got her all worked up. I had no idea she'd get out of bed to start building a fort for her stuffed animals while I was making the cupcakes."

"No worries," he said with a small chuckle. He wasn't surprised; he knew his five-year-old, Faith, well. "I'm prepared for massive crankiness tomorrow."

He saw her horrified look and wished he'd stayed silent. He didn't like seeing Elena Anderson upset. And every time he'd seen her that way, he'd had to fight the urge to pull her into his arms and kiss the worry right off her face.

And that definitely wasn't the direction his mind needed to be going. Not with her. Not with his boss and friend's daughter. And definitely not with his babysitter.

"Seriously," he said to reassure her, "it's no big deal. Kids stay up late. They sneak out of bed. It happens. And I really appreciate you helping me out. I know childcare wasn't what you had in mind when you started graduate school."

"I'm happy to help. Truly. She's a great kid, and since your schedule is flexible it's easy to be here when you need me. Most of the time I'm working on my own. You know how grad school is."

"I don't actually. Cop. Security specialist. Now bar owner and partner to your father," he added, because he really needed to say that out loud. A reminder to them both. Because even though he'd been telling himself for months that it was his imagination, he knew damn well that Elena was attracted to him, too.

Hell, lightning had positively crackled between them the first time they'd met. And more than once he'd caught her looking at him, the desire so palpable that he'd had to turn away and imagine cold showers and other non-sensual things.

He was a wreck, and he was quickly losing confidence in his excuse that because it had been so long since he'd had a woman in his bed, that he was starved for any woman.

She flashed a sweet, almost shy smile, and his stomach flip-flopped.

No. It was Elena. Definitely Elena.

"This is nice," she said. "Chatting, I mean. Usually I'm rushing off the second you get home."

"Well, I can't let you risk ruining the cupcakes."

"That's something else I'm sorry for. I should have called to clear it with you. So I hope you don't mind. Apparently she needs them for school."

"I don't mind at all. I just…"

"Yes?"

How could he say that the room seemed too small, but he knew damn well that it wasn't because of the heat from the oven?

"Nothing," he said instead. "Forgot what I was going to say."

She cocked her head, a question in her eyes, and for a second he thought she might be about to call him out on his lie. He almost hoped she would.

Bing!

"Done," she said, her voice a little too bright, as if that would combat the tension in the room.

She bent to take them out, and Brent forced himself not to study the perfect curve of her ass in her Lucky jeans.

Lucky. Wasn't that ironic?

She put the cupcake pan on a trivet, then took off the oven mitts. "Well. There. I guess I should get going."

"Don't they need to cool?"

She nodded. "I figure you've done this before, right? Faith can frost them in the morning. And you just need to put them in some Tupperware."

"Right. I could do that. Or you could stay and make sure I don't put them away too soon."

She swallowed. "Well, yeah. If that would help you out."

He took one step toward her, and in the small kitchen that put them only inches apart. "Or you could forget about the cupcakes and just stay."

"I—Brent." She licked her lips, and his whole body tightened with desire. "What are you doing?"

"Honestly? I'm thinking about kissing you."

"Oh." He saw both surprise and pleasure in her eyes. "What about it?"

"How much I want to. How much I shouldn't."

"Why not?" The question was breathy, almost a whisper.

"For one, you're younger than me. You're my boss's daughter. My friend's daughter. Not to mention that I'm a single dad who needs to be careful about the signals I send to my kid. Plus, you're the babysitter."

"Those are all bad?"

He sighed. "I thought so. I'm starting to lose perspective."

"I can help with that."

"Can you?"

"Yeah." She took a step toward him, then rose up on her tiptoes. Gently, she brushed a kiss over his lips.

Then she backed away, biting her lower lip as she looked at him, as if challenging him to do more.

Dammit, he took the challenge. Maybe he'd go straight to hell, but he had to have this woman. And without any more hesitation, he pulled her close, then claimed her mouth in a kiss the seared through him, long and hot and deep.

Are you eager to learn which Man of the Month book features which sexy hero? Here's a handy list!

Down On Me - meet Reece
Hold On Tight - meet Spencer
Need You Now - meet Cameron
Start Me Up - meet Nolan
Get It On - meet Tyree
In Your Eyes - meet Parker
Turn Me On - meet Derek
Shake It Up - meet Landon
All Night Long - meet Easton
In Too Deep - meet Matthew
Light My Fire - meet Griffin
Walk The Line - meet Brent
&
Bar Bites: A Man of the Month Cookbook

Down On Me excerpt

Did you miss book one in the Man of the Month series? Here's an excerpt from Down On Me!

Chapter One

Reece Walker ran his palms over the slick, soapy ass of the woman in his arms and knew that he was going straight to hell.

Not because he'd slept with a woman he barely knew. Not because he'd enticed her into bed with a series of well-timed bourbons and particularly inventive half-truths. Not even because he'd lied to his best friend Brent about why Reece couldn't drive with him to the airport to pick up Jenna, the third player in their trifecta of lifelong friendship.

No, Reece was staring at the fiery pit because he was a lame, horny asshole without the balls to tell the naked beauty standing in the shower with him that she wasn't the woman he'd been thinking about for the last four hours.

And if that wasn't one of the pathways to hell, it damn sure ought to be.

He let out a sigh of frustration, and Megan tilted her head, one eyebrow rising in question as she slid her hand down to stroke his cock, which was demonstrating no guilt whatsoever about the whole going to hell issue. "Am I boring you?"

"Hardly." That, at least, was the truth. He felt like a prick, yes. But he was a well-satisfied one. "I was just thinking that you're beautiful."

She smiled, looking both shy and pleased—and Reece felt even more like a heel. What the devil was wrong with him? She *was* beautiful. And hot and funny and easy to talk to. Not to mention good in bed.

But she wasn't Jenna, which was a ridiculous comparison. Because Megan qualified as fair game, whereas Jenna was one of his two best friends. She trusted him. Loved him. And despite the way his cock perked up at the thought of doing all sorts of delicious things with her in bed, Reece knew damn well that would never happen. No way was he risking their friendship. Besides, Jenna didn't love him like that. Never had, never would.

And that—plus about a billion more reasons—meant that Jenna was entirely off-limits.

Too bad his vivid imagination hadn't yet gotten the memo.

Fuck it.

He tightened his grip, squeezing Megan's perfect rear. "Forget the shower," he murmured. "I'm taking you back to bed." He needed this. Wild. Hot. Demanding. And dirty enough to keep him from thinking.

Hell, he'd scorch the earth if that's what it took to burn Jenna from his mind—and he'd leave Megan limp, whimpering, and very, very satisfied. His guilt. Her pleasure. At least it would be a win for one of them.

And who knows? Maybe he'd manage to fuck the fantasies of his best friend right out of his head.

It didn't work.

Reece sprawled on his back, eyes closed, as Megan's gentle fingers traced the intricate outline of the tattoos inked across his pecs and down his arms. Her touch was warm and tender, in stark contrast to the way he'd just fucked her—a little too wild, a little too hard, as if he were fighting a battle, not making love.

Well, that was true, wasn't it?

But it was a battle he'd lost. Victory would have brought oblivion. Yet here he was, a naked woman beside him, and his thoughts still on Jenna, as wild and intense and impossible as they'd been since that night eight months ago when the earth had shifted beneath him, and he'd let himself look at her as a woman and not as a friend.

One breathtaking, transformative night, and Jenna didn't even realize it. And he'd be damned if he'd ever let her figure it out.

Beside him, Megan continued her exploration, one fingertip tracing the outline of a star. "No names? No wife or girlfriend's initials hidden in the design?"

He turned his head sharply, and she burst out laughing.

"Oh, don't look at me like that." She pulled the sheet up to cover her breasts as she rose to her knees beside him. "I'm just making conversation. No hidden agenda at all. Believe me, the last thing I'm interested in is a relationship." She scooted away, then sat on the edge of the bed, giving him an enticing view of her bare back. "I don't even do overnights."

As if to prove her point, she bent over, grabbed her bra off the floor, and started getting dressed.

"Then that's one more thing we have in common." He pushed himself up, rested his back against the headboard, and enjoyed the view as she wiggled into her jeans.

"Good," she said, with such force that he knew she meant it, and for a moment he wondered what had soured her on relationships.

As for himself, he hadn't soured so much as fizzled. He'd had a few serious girlfriends over the years, but it never worked out. No matter how good it started, invariably the relationship crumbled. Eventually, he had to acknowledge that he simply wasn't relationship material. But that didn't mean he was a monk, the last eight months notwithstanding.

She put on her blouse and glanced around, then slipped her feet into her shoes. Taking the hint, he got up and pulled on his jeans and T-shirt. "Yes?" he asked, noticing the way she was eying him speculatively.

"The truth is, I was starting to think you might be in a relationship."

"What? Why?"

She shrugged. "You were so quiet there for a while, I wondered if maybe I'd misjudged you. I thought you might be married and feeling guilty."

Guilty.

The word rattled around in his head, and he groaned. "Yeah, you could say that."

"Oh, *hell*. Seriously?"

"No," he said hurriedly. "Not that. I'm not cheating on my non-existent wife. I wouldn't. Not ever." Not in small part because Reece wouldn't ever have a wife since he thought the institution of marriage was a crock, but he didn't see the need to explain that to Megan.

"But as for guilt?" he continued. "Yeah, tonight I've got that in spades."

She relaxed slightly. "Hmm. Well, sorry about the guilt, but I'm glad about the rest. I have rules, and I consider myself a good judge of character. It makes me cranky when I'm wrong."

"Wouldn't want to make you cranky."

"Oh, you really wouldn't. I can be a total bitch." She sat on the edge of the bed and watched as he tugged on his boots. "But if you're not hiding a wife in your attic, what are you feeling guilty about? I assure you, if it has anything to do with my satisfaction, you needn't feel guilty at all." She flashed a mischievous grin, and he couldn't help but smile back. He hadn't invited a woman into his bed for eight long months. At least he'd had the good fortune to pick one he actually liked.

"It's just that I'm a crappy friend," he admitted.

"I doubt that's true."

"Oh, it is," he assured her as he tucked his wallet into his back pocket. The irony, of course, was that as far as Jenna knew, he was an excellent friend. The best. One of her two pseudo-brothers with whom she'd sworn a blood oath the summer after sixth grade, almost twenty years ago.

From Jenna's perspective, Reece was at least as good as Brent, even if the latter scored bonus points because he was picking Jenna up at the airport while Reece was trying to fuck his personal demons into oblivion. Trying anything, in fact, that would exorcise the memory of how she'd clung to him that night, her curves enticing and her breath intoxicating, and not just because of the scent of too much alcohol.

She'd trusted him to be the white knight, her noble rescuer, and all he'd been able to think about was the feel of her body, soft and warm against his, as he carried her up the stairs to her apartment.

A wild craving had hit him that night, like a tidal wave of emotion crashing over him, washing away the outer shell of friendship and leaving nothing but raw desire and a longing so potent it nearly brought him to his knees.

It had taken all his strength to keep his distance when the only thing he'd wanted was to cover every inch of her naked body with kisses. To stroke her skin and watch her writhe with pleasure.

He'd won a hard-fought battle when he reined in his desire that night. But his victory wasn't without its wounds. She'd pierced his heart when she'd drifted to sleep in his arms, whispering that she loved him—and he knew that she meant it only as a friend.

More than that, he knew that he was the biggest asshole to ever walk the earth.

Thankfully, Jenna remembered nothing of that night. The liquor had stolen her memories, leaving her with a monster hangover, and him with a Jenna-shaped hole in his heart.

"Well?" Megan pressed. "Are you going to tell me? Or do I have to guess?"

"I blew off a friend."

"Yeah? That probably won't score you points in the Friend of the Year competition, but it doesn't sound too dire. Unless you were the best man and blew off the wedding? Left someone stranded at the side of the road somewhere in West Texas? Or promised to feed their cat and totally forgot? Oh, God. Please tell me you didn't kill Fluffy."

He bit back a laugh, feeling slightly better. "A friend came in tonight, and I feel like a complete shit for not meeting her plane."

"Well, there are taxis. And I assume she's an adult?"

"She is, and another friend is there to pick her up."

"I see," she said, and the way she slowly nodded suggested that she saw too much. "I'm guessing that *friend* means *girlfriend*? Or, no. You wouldn't do that. So she must be an ex."

"Really not," he assured her. "Just a friend. Lifelong, since sixth grade."

"Oh, I get it. Longtime friend. High expectations. She's going to be pissed."

"Nah. She's cool. Besides, she knows I usually work nights."

"Then what's the problem?"

He ran his hand over his shaved head, the bristles from the day's growth like sandpaper against his palm. "Hell if I know," he lied, then forced a smile, because whether his problem was guilt or lust or just plain stupidity, she hardly deserved to be on the receiving end of his bullshit.

He rattled his car keys. "How about I buy you one last drink before I take you home?"

"You're sure you don't mind a working drink?" Reece asked as he helped Megan out of his cherished baby blue vintage Chevy pickup. "Normally I wouldn't take you to my job, but we just hired a new bar back, and I want to see how it's going."

He'd snagged one of the coveted parking spots on Sixth Street, about a block down from The Fix, and he glanced automatically toward the bar, the glow from the windows relaxing him. He didn't own the place, but it was like a second home to him and had been for one hell of a long time.

"There's a new guy in training, and you're not there? I thought you told me you were the manager?"

"I did, and I am, but Tyree's there. The owner, I mean. He's always on site when someone new is starting. Says it's his job, not mine. Besides,

Sunday's my day off, and Tyree's a stickler for keeping to the schedule."

"Okay, but why are you going then?"

"Honestly? The new guy's my cousin. He'll probably give me shit for checking in on him, but old habits die hard." Michael had been almost four when Vincent died, and the loss of his dad hit him hard. At sixteen, Reece had tried to be stoic, but Uncle Vincent had been like a second father to him, and he'd always thought of Mike as more brother than cousin. Either way, from that day on, he'd made it his job to watch out for the kid.

"Nah, he'll appreciate it," Megan said. "I've got a little sister, and she gripes when I check up on her, but it's all for show. She likes knowing I have her back. And as for getting a drink where you work, I don't mind at all."

As a general rule, late nights on Sunday were dead, both in the bar and on Sixth Street, the popular downtown Austin street that had been a focal point of the city's nightlife for decades. Tonight was no exception. At half-past one in the morning, the street was mostly deserted. Just a few cars moving slowly, their headlights shining toward the west, and a smattering of couples, stumbling and laughing. Probably tourists on their way back to one of the downtown hotels.

It was late April, though, and the spring weather was drawing both locals and tourists. Soon, the area —and the bar—would be bursting at the seams. Even on a slow Sunday night.

Situated just a few blocks down from Congress Avenue, the main downtown artery, The Fix on Sixth attracted a healthy mix of tourists and locals. The bar had existed in one form or another for decades, becoming a local staple, albeit one that had been falling deeper and deeper into disrepair until Tyree had bought the place six years ago and started it on much-needed life support.

"You've never been here before?" Reece asked as he paused in front of the oak and glass doors etched with the bar's familiar logo.

"I only moved downtown last month. I was in Los Angeles before."

The words hit Reece with unexpected force. Jenna had been in LA, and a wave of both longing and regret crashed over him. He should have gone with Brent. What the hell kind of friend was he, punishing Jenna because he couldn't control his own damn libido?

With effort, he forced the thoughts back. He'd already beaten that horse to death.

"Come on," he said, sliding one arm around her shoulder and pulling open the door with his other. "You're going to love it."

He led her inside, breathing in the familiar mix of alcohol, southern cooking, and something indiscernible he liked to think of as the scent of a damn good time. As he expected, the place was mostly empty. There was no live music on Sunday nights, and at less than an hour to closing, there were only three customers in the front room.

"Megan, meet Cameron," Reece said, pulling out a stool for her as he nodded to the bartender in introduction. Down the bar, he saw Griffin Draper, a regular, lift his head, his face obscured by his hoodie, but his attention on Megan as she chatted with Cam about the house wines.

Reece nodded hello, but Griffin turned back to his notebook so smoothly and nonchalantly that Reece wondered if maybe he'd just been staring into space, thinking, and hadn't seen Reece or Megan at all. That was probably the case, actually. Griff wrote a popular podcast that had been turned into an even more popular web series, and when he wasn't recording the dialogue, he was usually writing a script.

"So where's Mike? With Tyree?"

Cameron made a face, looking younger than his twenty-four years. "Tyree's gone."

"You're kidding. Did something happen with Mike?" His cousin was a responsible kid. Surely he hadn't somehow screwed up his first day on the job.

"No, Mike's great." Cam slid a Scotch in front of Reece. "Sharp, quick, hard worker. He went off the clock about an hour ago, though. So you just missed him."

"Tyree shortened his shift?"

Cam shrugged. "Guess so. Was he supposed to be on until closing?"

"Yeah." Reece frowned. "He was. Tyree say why he cut him loose?"

"No, but don't sweat it. Your cousin's fitting right in. Probably just because it's Sunday and slow. " He made a face. "And since Tyree followed him out, guess who's closing for the first time alone."

"So you're in the hot seat, huh? " Reece tried to sound casual. He was standing behind Megan's stool, but now he moved to lean against the bar, hoping his casual posture suggested that he wasn't worried at all. He was, but he didn't want Cam to realize it. Tyree didn't leave employees to close on their own. Not until he'd spent weeks training them.

"I told him I want the weekend assistant manager position. I'm guessing this is his way of seeing how I work under pressure."

"Probably," Reece agreed half-heartedly. "What did he say?"

"Honestly, not much. He took a call in the office, told Mike he could head home, then about fifteen minutes later said he needed to take off, too, and that I was the man for the night."

"Trouble?" Megan asked.

"No. Just chatting up my boy," Reece said, surprised at how casual his voice sounded. Because the scenario had trouble printed all over it. He just wasn't sure what kind of trouble.

He focused again on Cam. "What about the wait-staff?" Normally, Tiffany would be in the main bar taking care of the customers who sat at tables. "He didn't send them home, too, did he?"

"Oh, no," Cam said. "Tiffany and Aly are scheduled to be on until closing, and they're in the back with—"

But his last words were drowned out by a high-pitched squeal of "*You're here!*" and Reece looked up to find Jenna Montgomery—the woman he craved —barreling across the room and flinging herself into his arms.

Meet Damien Stark

Only his passion could set her free…

Release Me
Claim Me
Complete Me
Anchor Me
Lost With Me

Meet Damien Stark in Release Me, *book 1 of the wildly sensual series that's left millions of readers breathless …*

Chapter One

A cool ocean breeze caresses my bare shoulders,

and I shiver, wishing I'd taken my roommate's advice and brought a shawl with me tonight. I arrived in Los Angeles only four days ago, and I haven't yet adjusted to the concept of summer temperatures changing with the setting of the sun. In Dallas, June is hot, July is hotter, and August is hell.

Not so in California, at least not by the beach. LA Lesson Number One: Always carry a sweater if you'll be out after dark.

Of course, I could leave the balcony and go back inside to the party. Mingle with the millionaires. Chat up the celebrities. Gaze dutifully at the paintings. It is a gala art opening, after all, and my boss brought me here to meet and greet and charm and chat. Not to lust over the panorama that is coming alive in front of me. Bloodred clouds bursting against the pale orange sky. Blue-gray waves shimmering with dappled gold.

I press my hands against the balcony rail and lean forward, drawn to the intense, unreachable beauty of the setting sun. I regret that I didn't bring the battered Nikon I've had since high school. Not that it would have fit in my itty-bitty beaded purse. And a bulky camera bag paired with a little black dress is a big, fat fashion no-no.

But this is my very first Pacific Ocean sunset, and I'm determined to document the moment. I pull out my iPhone and snap a picture.

"Almost makes the paintings inside seem redundant, doesn't it?" I recognize the throaty, feminine voice and turn to face Evelyn Dodge, retired actress turned agent turned patron of the arts—and my hostess for the evening.

"I'm so sorry. I know I must look like a giddy tourist, but we don't have sunsets like this in Dallas."

"Don't apologize," she says. "I pay for that view every month when I write the mortgage check. It damn well better be spectacular."

I laugh, immediately more at ease.

"Hiding out?"

"Excuse me?"

"You're Carl's new assistant, right?" she asks, referring to my boss of three days.

"Nikki Fairchild."

"I remember now. Nikki from Texas." She looks me up and down, and I wonder if she's disappointed that I don't have big hair and cowboy boots. "So who does he want you to charm?"

"Charm?" I repeat, as if I don't know exactly what she means.

She cocks a single brow. "Honey, the man would rather walk on burning coals than come to an art show. He's fishing for investors and you're the bait." She makes a rough noise in the back of her throat. "Don't worry. I won't press you to tell me who. And I don't blame you for hiding out. Carl's brilliant, but he's a bit of a prick."

"It's the brilliant part I signed on for," I say, and she barks out a laugh.

The truth is that she's right about me being the bait. "Wear a cocktail dress," Carl had said. "Something flirty."

Seriously? I mean, *Seriously?*

I should have told him to wear his own damn cocktail dress. But I didn't. Because I want this job. I fought to get this job. Carl's company, C-Squared Technologies, successfully launched three web-based products in the last eighteen months. That track record had caught the industry's eye, and Carl had been hailed as a man to watch.

More important from my perspective, that meant he was a man to learn from, and I'd prepared for the job interview with an intensity bordering on obsession. Landing the position had been a huge coup for me. So what if he wanted me to wear something flirty? It was a small price to pay.

Shit.

"I need to get back to being the bait," I say.

"Oh, hell. Now I've gone and made you feel either guilty or self-conscious. Don't be. Let them get liquored up in there first. You catch more flies with alcohol anyway. Trust me. I know."

She's holding a pack of cigarettes, and now she taps one out, then extends the pack to me. I shake my head. I love the smell of tobacco—it reminds me of my grandfather—but actually inhaling the smoke does nothing for me.

"I'm too old and set in my ways to quit," she says. "But God forbid I smoke in my own damn house. I swear, the mob would burn me in effigy. You're not going to start lecturing me on the dangers of secondhand smoke, are you?"

"No," I promise.

"Then how about a light?"

I hold up the itty-bitty purse. "One lipstick, a credit card, my driver's license, and my phone."

"No condom?"

"I didn't think it was that kind of party," I say dryly.

"I knew I liked you." She glances around the balcony. "What the hell kind of party am I throwing if I don't even have one goddamn candle on one goddamn table? Well, fuck it." She puts the unlit cigarette to her mouth and inhales, her eyes closed and her expression rapturous. I can't help but like her. She wears hardly any makeup, in stark contrast to all the other women here tonight, myself included, and her dress is more of a caftan, the batik pattern as interesting as the woman herself.

She's what my mother would call a brassy broad—

loud, large, opinionated, and self-confident. My mother would hate her. I think she's awesome.

She drops the unlit cigarette onto the tile and grinds it with the toe of her shoe. Then she signals to one of the catering staff, a girl dressed all in black and carrying a tray of champagne glasses.

The girl fumbles for a minute with the sliding door that opens onto the balcony, and I imagine those flutes tumbling off, breaking against the hard tile, the scattered shards glittering like a wash of diamonds.

I picture myself bending to snatch up a broken stem. I see the raw edge cutting into the soft flesh at the base of my thumb as I squeeze. I watch myself clutching it tighter, drawing strength from the pain, the way some people might try to extract luck from a rabbit's foot.

The fantasy blurs with memory, jarring me with its potency. It's fast and powerful, and a little disturbing because I haven't needed the pain in a long time, and I don't understand why I'm thinking about it now, when I feel steady and in control.

I am fine, I think. *I am fine, I am fine, I am fine.*

"Take one, honey," Evelyn says easily, holding a flute out to me.

I hesitate, searching her face for signs that my mask has slipped and she's caught a glimpse of my rawness. But her face is clear and genial.

"No, don't you argue," she adds, misinterpreting my hesitation. "I bought a dozen cases and I hate to see good alcohol go to waste. Hell no," she adds when the girl tries to hand her a flute. "I hate the stuff. Get me a vodka. Straight up. Chilled. Four olives. Hurry up, now. Do you want me to dry up like a leaf and float away?"

The girl shakes her head, looking a bit like a twitchy, frightened rabbit. Possibly one that had sacrificed his foot for someone else's good luck.

Evelyn's attention returns to me. "So how do you like LA? What have you seen? Where have you been? Have you bought a map of the stars yet? Dear God, tell me you're not getting sucked into all that tourist bullshit."

"Mostly I've seen miles of freeway and the inside of my apartment."

"Well, that's just sad. Makes me even more glad

that Carl dragged your skinny ass all the way out here tonight."

I've put on fifteen welcome pounds since the years when my mother monitored every tiny thing that went in my mouth, and while I'm perfectly happy with my size-eight ass, I wouldn't describe it as skinny. I know Evelyn means it as a compliment, though, and so I smile. "I'm glad he brought me, too. The paintings really are amazing."

"Now don't do that—don't you go sliding into the polite-conversation routine. No, no," she says before I can protest. "I'm sure you mean it. Hell, the paintings are wonderful. But you're getting the flat-eyed look of a girl on her best behavior, and we can't have that. Not when I was getting to know the real you."

"Sorry," I say. "I swear I'm not fading away on you."

Because I genuinely like her, I don't tell her that she's wrong—she hasn't met the real Nikki Fairchild. She's met Social Nikki who, much like Malibu Barbie, comes with a complete set of accessories. In my case, it's not a bikini and a convertible.

Instead, I have the *Elizabeth Fairchild Guide for Social Gatherings*.

My mother's big on rules. She claims it's her Southern upbringing. In my weaker moments, I agree. Mostly, I just think she's a controlling bitch. Since the first time she took me for tea at the Mansion at Turtle Creek in Dallas at age three, I have had the rules drilled into my head. How to walk, how to talk, how to dress. What to eat, how much to drink, what kinds of jokes to tell.

I have it all down, every trick, every nuance, and I wear my practiced pageant smile like armor against the world. The result being that I don't think I could truly be myself at a party even if my life depended on it.

This, however, is not something Evelyn needs to know.

"Where exactly are you living?" she asks.

"Studio City. I'm sharing a condo with my best friend from high school."

"Straight down the 101 for work and then back home again. No wonder you've only seen concrete.

Didn't anyone tell you that you should have taken an apartment on the Westside?"

"Too pricey to go it alone," I admit, and I can tell that my admission surprises her. When I make the effort—like when I'm Social Nikki—I can't help but look like I come from money. Probably because I do. Come from it, that is. But that doesn't mean I brought it with me.

"How old are you?"

"Twenty-four."

Evelyn nods sagely, as if my age reveals some secret about me. "You'll be wanting a place of your own soon enough. You call me when you do and we'll find you someplace with a view. Not as good as this one, of course, but we can manage something better than a freeway on-ramp."

"It's not that bad, I promise."

"Of course it's not," she says in a tone that says the exact opposite. "As for views," she continues, gesturing toward the now-dark ocean and the sky that's starting to bloom with stars, "you're welcome to come back anytime and share mine."

"I might take you up on that," I admit. "I'd love to

bring a decent camera back here and take a shot or two."

"It's an open invitation. I'll provide the wine and you can provide the entertainment. A young woman loose in the city. Will it be a drama? A rom-com? Not a tragedy, I hope. I love a good cry as much as the next woman, but I like you. You need a happy ending."

I tense, but Evelyn doesn't know she's hit a nerve. That's why I moved to LA, after all. New life. New story. New Nikki.

I ramp up the Social Nikki smile and lift my champagne flute. "To happy endings. And to this amazing party. I think I've kept you from it long enough."

"Bullshit," she says. "I'm the one monopolizing you, and we both know it."

We slip back inside, the buzz of alcohol-fueled conversation replacing the soft calm of the ocean.

"The truth is, I'm a terrible hostess. I do what I want, talk to whoever I want, and if my guests feel slighted they can damn well deal with it."

I gape. I can almost hear my mother's cries of horror all the way from Dallas.

"Besides," she continues, "this party isn't supposed to be about me. I put together this little shindig to introduce Blaine and his art to the community. He's the one who should be doing the mingling, not me. I may be fucking him, but I'm not going to baby him."

Evelyn has completely destroyed my image of how a hostess for the not-to-be-missed social event of the weekend is supposed to behave, and I think I'm a little in love with her for that.

"I haven't met Blaine yet. That's him, right?" I point to a tall reed of a man. He is bald, but sports a red goatee. I'm pretty sure it's not his natural color. A small crowd hums around him, like bees drawing nectar from a flower. His outfit is certainly as bright as one.

"That's my little center of attention, all right," Evelyn says. "The man of the hour. Talented, isn't he?" Her hand sweeps out to indicate her massive living room. Every wall is covered with paintings. Except for a few benches, whatever furniture was once in the room has been removed and replaced with easels on which more paintings stand.

I suppose technically they are portraits. The models are nudes, but these aren't like anything you would see in a classical art book. There's something edgy about them. Something provocative and raw. I can tell that they are expertly conceived and carried out, and yet they disturb me, as if they reveal more about the person viewing the portrait than about the painter or the model.

As far as I can tell, I'm the only one with that reaction. Certainly the crowd around Blaine is glowing. I can hear the gushing praise from here.

"I picked a winner with that one," Evelyn says. "But let's see. Who do you want to meet? Rip Carrington and Lyle Tarpin? Those two are guaranteed drama, that's for damn sure, and your roommate will be jealous as hell if you chat them up."

"She will?"

Evelyn's brows arch up. "Rip and Lyle? They've been feuding for weeks." She narrows her eyes at me. "The fiasco about the new season of their sitcom? It's all over the Internet? You really don't know them?"

"Sorry," I say, feeling the need to apologize. "My school schedule was pretty intense. And I'm sure you can imagine what working for Carl is like."

Speaking of …

I glance around, but I don't see my boss anywhere.

"That is one serious gap in your education," Evelyn says. "Culture—and yes, pop culture counts—is just as important as—what did you say you studied?"

"I don't think I mentioned it. But I have a double major in electrical engineering and computer science."

"So you've got brains and beauty. See? That's something else we have in common. Gotta say, though, with an education like that, I don't see why you signed up to be Carl's secretary."

I laugh. "I'm not, I swear. Carl was looking for someone with tech experience to work with him on the business side of things, and I was looking for a job where I could learn the business side. Get my feet wet. I think he was a little hesitant to hire me at first—my skills definitely lean toward tech—but I convinced him I'm a fast learner."

She peers at me. "I smell ambition."

I lift a shoulder in a casual shrug. "It's Los Angeles. Isn't that what this town is all about?"

"Ha! Carl's lucky he's got you. It'll be interesting to see how long he keeps you. But let's see … who here would intrigue you …?"

She casts about the room, finally pointing to a fifty-something man holding court in a corner. "That's Charles Maynard," she says. "I've known Charlie for years. Intimidating as hell until you get to know him. But it's worth it. His clients are either celebrities with name recognition or power brokers with more money than God. Either way, he's got all the best stories."

"He's a lawyer?"

"With Bender, Twain & McGuire. Very prestigious firm."

"I know," I say, happy to show that I'm not entirely ignorant, despite not knowing Rip or Lyle. "One of my closest friends works for the firm. He started here but he's in their New York office now."

"Well, come on, then, Texas. I'll introduce you." We take one step in that direction, but then Evelyn stops me. Maynard has pulled out his phone, and is shouting instructions at someone. I catch a few well-placed curses and eye Evelyn sideways. She looks unconcerned "He's a pussycat at heart. Trust me, I've worked with him before. Back in my agenting days, we put together more celebrity biopic deals for our clients than I can count. And we fought to keep a few tell-alls off the screen, too." She shakes her head, as if reliving those glory days, then pats my arm. "Still, we'll wait 'til he calms down a bit. In the meantime, though …"

She trails off, and the corners of her mouth turn down in a frown as she scans the room again. "I don't think he's here yet, but—oh! Yes! Now *there's* someone you should meet. And if you want to talk views, the house he's building has one that makes my view look like, well, like yours." She points toward the entrance hall, but all I see are bobbing heads and haute couture. "He hardly ever accepts invitations, but we go way back," she says.

I still can't see who she's talking about, but then the crowd parts and I see the man in profile. Goose bumps rise on my arms, but I'm not cold. In fact, I'm suddenly very, very warm.

He's tall and so handsome that the word is almost an insult. But it's more than that. It's not his looks, it's his *presence*. He commands the room simply by being in it, and I realize that Evelyn and I aren't the only ones looking at him. The entire crowd has noticed his arrival. He must feel the weight of all those eyes, and yet the attention doesn't faze him at all. He smiles at the girl with the champagne, takes a glass, and begins to chat casually with a woman who approaches him, a simpering smile stretched across her face.

"Damn that girl," Evelyn says. "She never did bring me my vodka."

But I barely hear her. "Damien Stark," I say. My voice surprises me. It's little more than breath.

Evelyn's brows rise so high I notice the movement in my peripheral vision. "Well, how about that?" she says knowingly. "Looks like I guessed right."

"You did," I admit. "Mr. Stark is just the man I want to see."

I hope you enjoyed the excerpt! Grab your own copy of Release Me ... or any of the books in the series now!

The Original Trilogy

Release Me

Claim Me

Complete Me

And Beyond...

Anchor Me

Lost With Me

Some rave reviews for J. Kenner's sizzling romances...

I just get sucked into these books and can not get enough of this series. They are so well written and as satisfying as each book is they leave you greedy for more. — Goodreads reviewer on *Wicked Torture*

A sizzling, intoxicating, sexy read!!!! J. Kenner had me devouring Wicked Dirty, the second installment of *Stark World Series* in one sitting. I loved everything about this book from the opening pages to the raw and vulnerable characters. With her sophisticated prose, Kenner created a love story that had the perfect blend of lust, passion, sexual tension, raw emotions and love. - Michelle, Four Chicks Flipping Pages

Wicked Dirty CLAIMED and CONSUMED every ounce of me from the very first page. Mind racing. Pulse pounding. Breaths bated. Feels flowing. Eyes wide in anticipation. Heart beating out of my chest. I felt the current of *Wicked Dirty* flow through me. I was DRUNK on this book that was my fine whiskey, so smooth and spectacular, and could not get enough of this *Wicked Dirty* drink. - Karen Bookalicious Babes Blog

"Sinfully sexy and full of heart. Kenner shines in this second chance, slow burn of a romance. Wicked Grind is the perfect book to kick off your summer."- *K. Bromberg, New York Times bestselling author (on Wicked Grind)*

"J. Kenner never disappoints~her books just get better and better." - *Mom's Guilty Pleasure (on Wicked Grind)*

"I don't think J. Kenner could write a bad story if she tried. ... Wicked Grind is a great beginning to what I'm positive will be a very successful series. ... The line forms here." *iScream Books (On Wicked Grind)*

"Scorching, sweet, and soul-searing, *Anchor Me* is the ultimate love story that stands the test of time and tribulation. THE TRUEST LOVE!" *Bookalicious Babes Blog (on Anchor Me)*

"J. Kenner has brought this couple to life and the character connection that I have to these two holds no bounds and that is testament to J.

Kenner's writing ability." *The Romance Cover (on Anchor Me)*

"J. Kenner writes an emotional and personal story line. ... The premise will captivate your imagination; the characters will break your heart; the romance continues to push the envelope." *The Reading Café (on Anchor Me)*

"Kenner may very well have cornered the market on sinfully attractive, dominant antiheroes and the women who swoon for them . . ." *Romantic Times*

"*Wanted* is another J. Kenner masterpiece . . . This was an intriguing look at self-discovery and forbidden love all wrapped into a neat little action-suspense package. There was plenty of sexual tension and eventually action. Evan was hot, hot, hot! Together, they were combustible. But can we expect anything less from J. Kenner?" *Reading Haven*

"*Wanted* by J. Kenner is the whole package! A toe-curling smokin' hot read, full of incredible characters and a brilliant storyline that you won't be able to get enough of. I can't wait for the next book in this series . . . I'm hooked!" *Flirty & Dirty Book Blog*

"J. Kenner's evocative writing thrillingly captures the power of physical attraction, the pull of longing, the universe-altering effect one person can have on another. . . . *Claim Me* has the emotional depth to back up the sex . . . Every scene is infused with both erotic tension, and the tension of wondering what lies beneath Damien's veneer – and how and when it will be revealed." *Heroes and Heartbreakers*

"*Claim Me* by J. Kenner is an erotic, sexy and exciting ride. The story between Damien and Nikki is amazing and written beautifully. The intimate and detailed sex scenes will leave you fanning yourself to cool down. With the writing style of Ms. Kenner you almost feel like you are there in the story riding along the emotional rollercoaster with Damien and Nikki." *Fresh Fiction*

"PERFECT for fans of *Fifty Shades of Grey* and *Bared to You*. *Release Me* is a powerful and erotic romance novel that is sure to make adult romance readers sweat, sigh and swoon." *Reading, Eating & Dreaming Blog*

"I will admit, I am in the 'I loved *Fifty Shades*' camp,

but after reading *Release Me*, Mr. Grey only scratches the surface compared to Damien Stark." *Cocktails and Books Blog*

"It is not often when a book is so amazingly well-written that I find it hard to even begin to accurately describe it . . . I recommend this book to everyone who is interested in a passionate love story." *Romancebookworm's Reviews*

"The story is one that will rank up with the *Fifty Shades* and Cross Fire trilogies." *Incubus Publishing Blog*

"The plot is complex, the characters engaging, and J. Kenner's passionate writing brings it all perfectly together." *Harlequin Junkie*

Also by J. Kenner

The Stark Saga Novels:

Only his passion could set her free…

Meet Damien Stark

The Original Trilogy

Release Me

Claim Me

Complete Me

And Beyond…

Anchor Me

Lost With Me

Stark Ever After

(Stark Saga novellas):

Happily ever after is just the beginning.

The passion between Damien & Nikki continues.

Take Me

Have Me

Play My Game

Seduce Me

Unwrap Me

Deepest Kiss

Entice Me

Hold Me

Please Me

The Steele Books/Stark International:

He was the only man who made her feel alive.

Say My Name

On My Knees

Under My Skin

Take My Dare (includes short story Steal My Heart)

Stark International Novellas:

Meet Jamie & Ryan-so hot it sizzles.

Tame Me

Tempt Me

S.I.N. Trilogy:

It was wrong for them to be together...

...but harder to stay apart.

Dirtiest Secret

Hottest Mess

Sweetest Taboo

Stand alone novels:

Most Wanted:

Three powerful, dangerous men.

Three sensual, seductive women.

Wanted

Heated

Ignited

Wicked Nights (Stark World):

Sometimes it feels so damn good to be bad.

Wicked Grind

Wicked Dirty

Wicked Torture

Man of the Month

Who's your man of the month …?

Down On Me

Hold On Tight

Need You Now

Start Me Up

Get It On

In Your Eyes

Turn Me On

Shake It Up

All Night Long

In Too Deep

Light My Fire

Walk The Line

Bar Bites: A Man of the Month Cookbook(by J. Kenner & Suzanne M. Johnson)

Additional Titles

Wild Thing

One Night (A Stark World short story in the Second Chances anthology)

Also by Julie Kenner

The Protector (Superhero) Series:

The Cat's Fancy (prequel)

Aphrodite's Kiss

Aphrodite's Passion

Aphrodite's Secret

Aphrodite's Flame

Aphrodite's Embrace (novella)

Aphrodite's Delight (novella – free download)

Demon Hunting Soccer Mom Series:

Carpe Demon

California Demon

Demons Are Forever

Deja Demon

The Demon You Know (short story)

Demon Ex Machina

Pax Demonica

Day of the Demon

The Dark Pleasures Series:

Caress of Darkness

Find Me In Darkness

Find Me In Pleasure

Find Me In Passion

Caress of Pleasure

The Blood Lily Chronicles:

Tainted

Torn

Turned

Rising Storm:

Rising Storm: Tempest Rising

Rising Storm: Quiet Storm

Devil May Care:

Seducing Sin

Tempting Fate

About the Author

J. Kenner (aka Julie Kenner) is the *New York Times*, *USA Today*, *Publishers Weekly*, *Wall Street Journal* and #1 International bestselling author of over one hundred novels, novellas and short stories in a variety of genres.

JK has been praised by *Publishers Weekly* as an author with a "flair for dialogue and eccentric characterizations" and by *RT Bookclub* for having "cornered the market on sinfully attractive, dominant antiheroes and the women who swoon for them." A six-time finalist for Romance Writers of America's prestigious RITA award, JK took home the first RITA trophy awarded in the category of erotic romance in 2014 for her novel, *Claim Me* (book 2 of her Stark Trilogy).

In her previous career as an attorney, JK worked as a lawyer in Southern California and Texas. She currently lives in Central Texas, with her husband, two daughters, and two rather spastic cats.

More ways to connect:

www.jkenner.com

Text JKenner to 21000 for JK's text alerts.

 facebook.com/jkennerbooks

twitter.com/juliekenner

Made in the USA
Middletown, DE
13 July 2018